MAYHEM AT THE MOUNTAIN RESORT

CINDY BELL

Copyright © 2022 Cindy Bell

All rights reserved.

Cover Design by Lou Harper, Cover Affairs

All rights reserved. No part of this publication may be reproduced or transmitted in any form or by any means, electronic or mechanical, including photocopy, recording, or any information storage or retrieval system, without permission in writing from the publisher.

This is a work of fiction. The characters, incidents and locations portrayed in this book and the names herein are fictitious. Any similarity to or identification with the locations, names, characters or history of any person, product or entity is entirely coincidental and unintentional.

All trademarks and brands referred to in this book are for illustrative purposes only, are the property of their respective owners and not affiliated with this publication in any way. Any trademarks are being used without permission, and the publication of the trademark is not authorized by, associated with or sponsored by the trademark owner.

ISBN: 9798867601812

CHAPTER 1

Fresh mountain air flooded Samantha Smith's senses as she walked through the mountain resort, past the pool and tennis courts, toward a sprawling, three-story building. The sound of the leaves rustling drifted toward her from the woods. Already, a sense of rejuvenation rushed through her veins. It was sunny and quite warm for a fall day.

Beyond the two large, wooden doors that stood in the center of the lodge, she sensed the potential for an exciting experience.

The brick exterior paired with dark-green shutters and an abundance of planters, struck her as quaint and inviting. She smiled as she recalled her resistance to taking the trip. It wasn't often that she did anything on her own. With a good group of friends in the retirement community of Sage Gardens, she almost always had a companion. But when the opportunity had come up for a chance to tour and review the Junction Mountain Resort, she decided to strike out on her own. Although she was a former crime journalist, it had been a long time since she'd written a piece to be published, and the offer had sparked her creative juices.

"I'm glad I came already," Samantha muttered to herself as she pulled open the front door and was greeted by a strong scent of cinnamon and apples that drifted through the air. The lobby was exactly what she expected to find in the cozy mountain retreat, with thick carpeting, a large fireplace, and plush, oversized furniture throughout. Instantly, she pictured herself curled up in one of the large chairs near the fireplace with a book.

Samantha sighed as her muscles relaxed. In the comfort of the surroundings, the tension of the flight and busy airport vanished, replaced with a faint buzz of excitement. She approached the front desk, eager to discover if the staff would be as pleasant as the surroundings already appeared to be.

"Hello, there." A man in a gray suit with a warm smile and thick, blond hair swept back from his broad forehead, met her eyes as she walked up. "Welcome to the Junction Mountain Resort. I'm so glad that you're here."

"Thanks." Samantha couldn't help but smile in return as his words seemed to be infused with genuine kindness. "I'm glad to be here." She gave him her information.

As he began the check-in process, she couldn't help but notice the striking blue color of his eyes and the athletic frame his tailored suit accentuated. He handed her a small welcome envelope and a key.

"Samantha, thanks for deciding to stay with us. The envelope has all of the information about our activities, and local events. Also, it includes a list of resources you might need during your stay here as well as some information about the town of Junction. My name is Kent. I'm the manager here, and if you have any questions at all, I'm more than happy to help. My number is included in the information, and you can call or text at any time."

"That's wonderful. Thank you so much. I didn't expect such personal service." Samantha eyed him for a moment as suspicion built within her. Did he somehow know that she was there to review the resort? Was that why he was treating her with such kindness?

"Customer service is our top priority here. If our guests aren't enjoying themselves, then we're doing something wrong." Kent smiled at her. "So, please don't hesitate to let me know if you need anything."

"I'm sure I won't need much." Samantha began to gather her purse, then glanced toward the front door as it swung open.

A woman, perhaps about ten years older than

Samantha, struggled to fit through with her sizable bags. Compared to the size of the bags she carried, the woman appeared quite small. She wore a colorful dress paired with high heels.

Samantha rushed toward her at the same moment that Kent rounded the desk and hurried in her direction.

"Let me help you with those." Kent began to take her bags before Samantha could reach the woman.

Samantha hung back and watched as the flustered woman patted down the stylish hat she wore. Red, with black lace, and a peacock feather perched on top.

"Thank you so much, what a gentleman." The woman waved her hand in front of her face and sighed. "It's so refreshing to know that there are still fine people in the world."

Just from the look of her, Samantha got the impression that she would be an entertaining person. The woman took a moment to fluff her hair, then proceeded forward. She carried herself with confidence, and perhaps a little arrogance.

As she flounced her way over to the front counter, she locked her eyes on to Kent. Samantha couldn't hold back a smile as she noticed the pink in the woman's cheeks and the way she pursed her lips.

She found herself fixated on the woman's movements. She did have a tendency to people watch. And this woman, whoever she was, appeared to be someone who would be quite interesting to watch. She decided to linger near the counter despite having everything that she needed.

As Samantha stepped to the side, she noticed another woman settle into one of the chairs in the lobby. She appeared to be in her twenties, and although she held a book in her hand, her eyes remained riveted on Kent. Samantha guessed that with his charming way and looks, he had the attention of most of the women who entered the resort. She pretended to search through her purse for something as Kent set the other woman's bags down beside the front desk.

Samantha glanced up and noticed the older woman's eyes following Kent as he walked around to the other side of the desk. She had a smile plastered across her lips.

Slightly shocked, but also very amused, Samantha focused on the pair, eager to see what might happen next.

CHAPTER 2

Still flustered from carrying her bags through the door, Cora Bing adjusted her hat. She noticed Kent's striking features as she followed him up to the front desk. He certainly was a handsome man, from his ice-blue eyes to his chiseled jaw and muscular frame.

"I'd like to check in please. Mrs. Cora Bing." She set her purse on the counter, then looked over at the woman beside her, with a light smile. Already, she had a good feeling about this vacation. Not only had she won it, which was a wonderful stroke of luck, but the place looked beautiful, and the host was charming.

"Absolutely. Give me just a moment to process your information." Kent glanced up at her as he typed on the keyboard. "I'm so glad that you're here."

"Me, too." Cora smiled. "I've been so busy lately, there's always something to do in Blue River, someone

MAYHEM AT THE MOUNTAIN RESORT

to check in on, a party that needs attending. I'm looking forward to a nice, relaxing stay." She wished her friends Betty Cale and Pearl White had been able to join her, but they both had family visiting, and the dates of the vacation couldn't be changed.

"I'm sure we will be able to accommodate that." Kent hit a button, and some paperwork began to print, then he turned his attention to the other woman. "Samantha, there is a menu in your room. All of the meals are served in our dining room and are available through room service at any time."

"Thank you so much." Samantha smiled. "I'm sure I will be taking advantage of both."

Cora assessed the slightly younger woman with some interest. She had a bit of pluck to her. She could tell from the way she spoke and carried herself. She turned her attention back to Kent as he handed over some paperwork for her to sign.

"Thanks. It's a bit intimidating to be here alone, though. I'd much rather have some companionship." Cora looked up at him as her pen glided across the paper.

"Well, your room is right next to Samantha's." Kent set her room key down beside the paperwork. "I'm sure the two of you will see plenty of each other."

"How wonderful." Cora smiled.

"Make sure you contact reception if you need anything." Kent returned her smile and tapped her copy of the paperwork. "That number goes directly to my cell phone. If you have any issues that aren't solved by the staff, feel free to call me. If I'm not available, the night manager will help you. I do hope you enjoy your stay with us."

"I'm sure I will." Cora picked up the paperwork.

The front door of the lodge swung open, and two dogs burst in, followed by a woman who clung tightly to their leashes.

"Oh, look at you two!" Cora gasped at the same moment that Samantha released a squeal of appreciation.

"Gorgeous dogs!" Samantha cried out as she headed straight for them. "May I pet them?"

"Of course." The woman nodded. Her chestnut hair hung just below her earlobes in a bob that gave shape to her rounded face. She looked to be in her thirties. "This is Boomer and Bruce." She gestured from the golden dog to the white one. "I'm Penny. My brother, Lincoln, and I own this resort." She held tight to the dogs' leashes as the two other women pet and cooed at the dogs.

Samantha had done some background research on the resort and knew that siblings, Lincoln and Penny, had used their inheritance from their parents to build the resort together. They had a younger brother, Collin, but from what she understood, he didn't inherit anything when his parents passed on because he was too young at the time. Penny and Lincoln were made his guardians.

"They are so gorgeous." Samantha smiled at the energetic dogs with curly hair. "What are they?"

"Labradoodles." The woman nodded. "Labrador and Poodle mix."

"This resort is beautiful." Samantha glanced up at her and smiled. "How lucky you are to live here year-round."

"Quite lucky." Penny looked up at Kent. "Have you seen Collin? He's supposed to take the boys for grooming today."

"I haven't seen him yet, today." Kent cleared his throat, then stepped around the counter to greet the dogs. "How are my boys?" He crouched down as the dogs ran in circles around him. "Have they just been for a walk?"

"Yes." Penny nodded. "I took them for their afternoon walk early. They won't be back in time to walk later."

"Oh, they just love you, don't they?" Cora grinned as she watched the excited dogs run around Kent. "That's a sign of a good person, when dogs love you like that."

"Well, I had the luxury of helping to take care of them while Collin was away at hospitality school. I guess you could say that we've bonded." Kent ruffled the dogs' fur, then straightened up. "You haven't heard from your brother today, either?"

"He's always up to something." Penny rolled her eyes. "I thought we were out of this phase when he hit his twenties, but I guess not. Excuse me, ladies. I need to get these two ready for their salon appointment." She winked, then led the dogs away.

As Kent walked back around behind the counter, Cora noticed that he favored his right leg. The limp was barely noticeable, but she detected it right away.

"You run?" Cora asked Kent as she noticed a small gym bag on the floor with a pair of sneakers beside it.

"Yes, I usually run each morning." Kent nodded. "But I don't go very fast."

"Me neither." Cora grinned. In fact, she couldn't recall the last time she'd gone for a run.

"I'll have your bags taken up to your room." Kent turned to Samantha. "Do you have more bags that need to be transported?"

"No, this is it." Samantha gave the small bag that hung at her side a pat. "I do my best to travel light."

"Are you just staying overnight?" Cora's eyes widened as she looked at the small bag.

"No, I'll be here all week." Samantha shrugged. "I just don't need much. I plan to go for a few walks and spend a lot of time in one of those chairs." She pointed to one of the overstuffed chairs near the fireplace.

"Oh dear." Cora clucked her tongue. "Samantha, when you're on vacation in paradise, you have to be ready for anything. Why, Mr. Right could be right around the corner, or perhaps behind a desk." She cast a quick wink in Kent's direction.

He smiled again, so wide that the expression lit up his clear, blue eyes.

"Oh no, no!" Samantha shook her head firmly. "I'm not here for that. I am here strictly to relax. One hundred percent me time."

"We'll see." Cora grinned.

CHAPTER 3

Cora began walking toward the hall that led to her room. She glanced back to see Samantha following after her. "I like to stay open to all of the possibilities. Isn't it amazing when you realize that each moment in life is a new adventure?"

"Each moment is a new adventure," Samantha repeated as she stepped up beside her and matched her pace to Cora's. "What a wonderful sentiment. I guess I've never really thought of it that way before."

"Just now, we both came into this resort, and we had no idea what might happen next, and already it has led to the two of us meeting. Quite a nice adventure, I'd say." Cora paused in front of her door. "I'm glad I've had the chance to meet you, Samantha, and I do hope that we will see each other again."

"I'm glad as well, Mrs. Bing." Samantha raised her eyebrows. "Is that what you'd like me to call you?"

"It's what just about everyone calls me." Cora waved her hand. "But if you'd like, you can call me Cora."

"Thank you, but Mrs. Bing is fine. I can't wait to see those two dogs again. I'd forgotten how much I enjoy having animals around." Samantha smiled at the thought of perhaps getting a pet when she returned home.

"Oh, animals I'm used to!" Cora laughed. "Back home, one of my favorite companions is a pot-bellied pig!"

"A pig?" Samantha gasped, then laughed. "Well, that does sound like an adventure."

"Trust me, it always is." Cora grinned, then stepped into her room.

Samantha continued down the hallway to the next room. She slid the key into the lock and opened the door. She stepped inside and felt some relief as she closed the door. Cora seemed like a sweet woman, but her focus was to relax, not make a new friend who had plenty of advice to give. She tossed her bag down on the floor near the double bed, then plopped down on the edge of it. As she took in the sight of the room, she smiled to herself. It wasn't very large, but it had all of the homey touches that made her feel relaxed. A few potted plants, an assortment of books on a shelf, and a coffee maker available right in the room.

She had no doubt that she would be quite comfortable. But a pang of sadness struck her as the quiet settled around her. She already missed her friends back home in Sage Gardens. There wasn't much they didn't do together, and the thought of being away from them for a week made her a little nervous. But that was exactly why she was there alone. She needed the quiet and the calm to be able to produce her best work. At least, that was what she told herself when she booked the room. She dug out one of the books she had packed and stretched out across the bed. Work would have to wait, as she needed to see what happened in the next chapter. She wanted to find out who the murderer was.

Samantha's body sank into the soft mattress comfortably. With a fluffy pillow under her head, her neck relaxed. She began to drink in the words on the page. Minutes later, her stomach churned, then released a disruptive growl. She winced as she realized how long it had been since she'd eaten. The schedule she'd been given at check-in listed dinner in a couple of hours, but she couldn't wait that long. She grabbed her purse and headed out into the hall in search of a vending machine of some kind.

Samantha crept quietly past Cora's door, hoping not to attract her attention. She didn't want to hear more about romance just yet. As she made her way through the lobby, she realized there wasn't a single vending machine to be found. However, she noticed a sign that pointed the way to the kitchen. She recalled Kent advising her that anything on the menu was available, even outside of mealtimes. She guessed that the kitchen staff would be able to take her order in person. She paused near the front desk, hoping to confirm things with Kent before she asked the kitchen staff, but there was no sign of him or anyone else.

With a shrug, Samantha continued in the direction of the kitchen. As she neared the double doors that led off the hallway and into the kitchen, the sound of angry voices made her freeze. She could hear the bang of a pot as it struck metal, followed by a man's loud voice.

"I've told you before, you can't come in here and treat me like this!"

"I absolutely can, that's my job!" another man snapped back. "If I tell you to do something, I expect you to do it, not continue to do things exactly as you please!"

"I've worked here for almost three years! You've barely been here for one!" the first voice shouted back. "I am the chef. I take care of the kitchen. You have no business being in here, and no say over me!"

"I am the manager!" The second voice raised even further.

Samantha took a sharp breath. Kent's voice sounded nothing like it had when he'd greeted her. Instead, it sounded deeper, and rough around the edges, as if his temper was strained to breaking point.

"Not for long, you're not!" The other man laughed. "Now that Collin is back, Penny and Lincoln will be handing over your job real fast to their younger brother."

"That's not true, they want him to earn the position." Kent cleared his throat. "And it's none of your business. All that matters right now is that I am the manager of this resort, and you work under me. If I ask you to fold those napkins into swans, that's what you'll do, and if I ask you to make sure that every meal you send out has a side of extra sauce, that's what you'll do."

"We'll see about that." Another metallic bang echoed out into the hallway. "Get out of my kitchen."

Samantha ducked back against the wall as one of the kitchen doors began to swing open.

"Penny and Lincoln will be hearing about this! Mark my words, Billy, you're going to regret this!" Kent's thick, blond hair peeked just beyond the door as he started to step out.

Samantha gulped back another breath, then stepped around a corner, just out of sight of Kent. She heard the door swing closed behind him. Then she listened as heavy steps traveled back in the direction of the lobby.

Still starving, but deterred by the argument, Samantha decided she would order her dinner to her room instead of risking coming face-to-face with Billy.

CHAPTER 4

*C*ora had every intention of going to the dining room for dinner, but she found that she craved something sweet the moment she entered her room. She reached into her suitcase and brought out a small box of chocolates from Charlotte's Chocolate Heaven that the owner, Charlotte Sweet, and her granddaughter, Ally, had given her for her vacation.

She opened the box and popped a milk chocolate praline in her mouth. The taste immediately made her miss her friends back home, not to mention Arnold, Charlotte's pot-bellied pig, and Peaches, Ally's cat.

As the chocolate melted on her tongue, she decided on her plans for the following day. She would take an early morning walk through the woods. She set her alarm and decided to read before going for dinner.

She soon drifted off to sleep.

Cora's eyes fluttered, then the ceiling came into

view. Disoriented, she tried to figure out exactly where she was. She soon remembered that she was at the resort.

She peeked at the clock. "And I overslept." She sat up in bed.

Her walk would have to wait. She wanted to have breakfast first. She had missed dinner and was hungry. She selected her favorite dress, then took some time to work on her hair and makeup. She liked to look her best. When she was younger, she worried more about what others thought and meeting society's expectations, but as she neared her eighth decade, she discovered that she needed to do what made her happy. When an opportunity presented itself, she did her very best to seize it. She headed down the hall.

As Cora neared the lobby, she noticed a bit of a commotion. Staff members moved quickly in different directions. Some spoke into their phones, others spoke in hushed tones to each other. Concern weighed heavily in each of their expressions. She frowned as she neared the front desk and saw no one behind it. She paused there, thinking that Kent might be back from his run already and would show up. She wanted to find a good route to walk after breakfast and thought Kent would be able to suggest one, seeing as he ran the trails in the morning. Though there were a few staff members around, none noticed her.

"Lincoln," a man in a chef's uniform called out to a

man in a suit, who looked to be in his thirties, with short, brown hair.

Cora recalled that Lincoln was Penny's brother and co-owner of the resort. She looked around the room again.

"Samantha! Oh, Samantha!" Cora waved to the woman who stood near the fireplace. A book had been abandoned on a small table beside an overstuffed chair.

Samantha walked toward her, with that same look of concern.

"Morning." Samantha paused beside her. "It's a little chaotic around here this morning."

"I can see that." Cora shook her head as a young staff member brushed past her in his urgency to get behind the counter.

"May I help you, ma'am?" He offered a forced smile.

"I would like to speak to Kent, if he's available, thank you." Cora smiled.

"Yes, I think we all would." He nodded. "Unfortunately, no one knows where he is."

"Excuse me?" Cora narrowed her eyes. "What do you mean by that?"

"He was supposed to be here over an hour ago, but no one's seen him or been able to contact him," he explained.

"No one has been able to contact him?" Cora repeated his words, as if she couldn't quite believe them. Her eyes traveled to the spot she'd noticed the gym bag and sneakers the day before. Both were absent. "Well, of course, he's out on his run. He must just be a little late." She recalled that Kent said that he couldn't run very fast. "Hasn't anyone checked the running trails?"

"We're in the process of figuring everything out." He gave her a reassuring smile. "Please enjoy the complimentary breakfast in the dining room." He hurried away from the front desk, back to the small group of employees gathered near the front door.

"But haven't you looked for him?" Cora called after him, stunned by his lack of concern. "What if he's in some kind of trouble? Hasn't anyone tried to find him?" Her words fell into the empty space around her, with no response from any of the staff members. She felt a warm hand on her shoulder and turned to face Samantha. "Oh, Samantha, I think something terrible has happened!"

"Because Kent is missing?" Samantha nodded. "I don't think it's anything to be too concerned about." She rubbed her hands along her arms as she decided not to share the panic she'd seen in a few of the staff members' expressions. She guessed this didn't happen very often.

"Yes, because Kent is missing." Cora paced back and forth in front of the desk. "How could someone just go missing?"

"It happens sometimes." Samantha watched the

woman continue to pace. "Listen, I'm sure he's just fine. Maybe he just had a late night and fell asleep somewhere, and he hasn't made it home yet. That's all."

"I don't think so." Cora shook her head. "I don't think he would do something like that."

"You don't even know him. You just met him yesterday. We both did." Samantha studied her. "How can you have any idea about what he would or wouldn't do?"

"I don't have to know him, to know. I haven't lived this long without learning how to read people." Cora pursed her lips, then shook her head. "I can't just do nothing. I have to try to see if he's okay."

"Now, wait a minute." Samantha stepped in front of her as she tried to move around her. "Just where do you think you're going?"

"I'm going to look for Kent, of course!" Cora threw her hands in the air and groaned. "Haven't you been listening to me at all? He's in trouble. I have to find out what happened to him. What if something went wrong when he went on his run? He could be hurt and alone, thinking that no one will come to save him."

"Or he could be curled up in bed." Samantha clucked her tongue. "Please, be reasonable. There are people out looking for him. He will turn up, and everything will be just fine. You shouldn't let this ruin your vacation."

"Listen, you can believe what you want. Hopefully, I'm wrong and he's just fine, but I can't do nothing." Cora started toward the door of the lobby.

"Hold on," Samantha called out.

"I have to do something." Cora pushed the door open.

As the door swung shut, Samantha knew that Cora wouldn't rest until she found Kent. But she was unfamiliar with the area, and certainly not dressed for wandering through the wilderness. Yes, Samantha could let her go off on her own in search of Kent, but what if something happened to her? Would she ever be able to forgive herself?

With this on her mind, she followed after Cora, who she was almost certain was overreacting. She was determined to at least keep track of her.

As if she sensed Samantha's intentions, Cora moved faster than Samantha could have predicted.

"Cora, where are you even going?" Samantha quickened her pace to catch up with her. "You have no idea where he might be!"

"I know he goes for a run, and I know there are running trails this way. I researched it all last night. I was planning on going on an early morning walk this morning, but unfortunately, I overslept." Cora shook her head. "If only I hadn't overslept, maybe I would have caught up with him."

"I'm sure he's fine." Samantha reached the beginning of the trail. She hadn't expected her morning to be jump-started in such a physical way, and her feet ached at the thought of walking the long trail. She paused to take a breath.

"Let's go, slowpoke." Cora glanced over her shoulder at her.

"Just a minute, please." Samantha winced at how winded she felt. Perhaps regular exercise needed to be more of a priority.

"Oh, look!" Cora pointed to the end of the trail, which was muddy. "Shoe prints! I knew we were going in the right direction." She narrowed her eyes. "But there are two sets. I guess he isn't alone."

"I'm sure that plenty of people use this trail." Samantha straightened up and took another deep breath. "I'm ready now, let's go." She barely got the words out of her mouth before Cora took off along the trail.

"Kent!" Cora shouted as she hurried along the trail. "Kent! Are you out here?"

"What if he isn't?" Samantha peered through the foliage at the edge of the trail. The yellows and oranges of the leaves that were starting to change color were beautiful. "What if he's somewhere else entirely?"

"Then at least I'll know that I looked for him!" Cora nodded as she quickened her pace.

Samantha grumbled as she trudged her way after Cora. As they rounded a bend in the trail, all of the foliage on the left side disappeared, replaced by an open view of the lake below them. The edge of the ridge wrapped around for a short distance before disappearing into trees and bushes again. Fascinated by the view, Samantha stepped closer to the edge. She drew a deep breath of the mountain air and remembered for a brief moment that she'd embarked on the vacation to relax.

"Let's go! We'll never find him that way!" Cora stepped up beside Samantha.

"But look at this view, it's just amazing." Samantha began to say more, but her words were drowned out by Cora's scream.

CHAPTER 5

Samantha gasped at the same moment that Cora's scream vibrated beside her.

Cora's eyes were fixated on the body sprawled in a ditch at the bottom of the ridge in front of her. Of all the possibilities, she had never considered that they would actually find Kent's body. But there it was, lying in front of her, without a sign of life to it. She brushed past Samantha and ran down the path to get to the ditch.

"Mrs. Bing, wait!" Samantha waved her hand through the air. "Mrs. Bing, slow down! Be careful!"

The high-pitched tone of Samantha's voice signaled how worried she was, but Cora could not be stopped as she barreled forward, despite the stems of her high heels sinking into the mud. Another scream tore through her throat as she neared Kent's motionless body.

"Oh, Samantha, I think he's dead!" Cora gasped.

Cora's heart sank as she tried to accept the truth. The way that Kent's body was angled, and the blood pooled around his head, made it seem impossible that he could still be alive.

"Maybe there's a chance." Samantha crouched down beside him and pressed her fingers lightly against his wrist.

Cora held her breath as Samantha waited a few seconds.

"No," Samantha whispered as she looked up at Cora. "I'm sorry."

"No, no, no!" Cora screamed. "This just can't be!"

Another scream from above them drowned out her own. She glanced up toward the path and noticed that a few people had gathered there, including Penny and Lincoln.

"Mrs. Bing, I know this is shocking for you." Samantha frowned as she stepped closer to her.

"If I hadn't overslept, I might have gotten here sooner." Cora shook her head. "I might have been able to help him."

"I don't think that there's anything we could have done." Samantha met the woman's eyes.

"Maybe not." Cora's voice grew stern. "But we have to find out what happened to him."

"Yes, of course we do." Samantha glanced toward the path. "But first we have to handle Penny and Lincoln. They're coming this way."

MAYHEM AT THE MOUNTAIN RESORT

Cora straightened her shoulders as she composed herself. The initial shock of finding Kent was wearing off. What had happened was terrible, but she had to keep it together.

"What happened here?" Penny gasped as she reached the ditch.

"We're not sure just yet." Cora briefly met Penny's eyes and noticed the shock in her expression. Seconds later, chaos broke out around them. Sirens wailed in the distance, while staff members from the resort charged down the side of the mountain and surrounded Kent's body.

"Oh, Kent, poor Kent," Penny moaned as she crouched down beside him. "He was so young!"

Lincoln leaned over Kent's body.

"Kent, you served us well, young man. You did a fine job." He choked back a sob as he straightened up. "Penny, we should let him be. Come away from him." He held her elbow and guided her back away from Kent's body.

"You need to stay away from the scene." Cora gestured for them to step back, as the reality that this was a crime scene dawned on her.

She knew she needed to tell them not to trample through the mud, not to touch the body. She'd read enough detective novels and helped investigate a few murders back home to know to preserve the crime scene.

"Samantha?" Cora poked the woman, who stood

perfectly still, lightly on the shoulder. "Are you okay, dear?"

"I'm not sure." Samantha blinked slowly, then looked over at Cora. "Are you?"

"I'm fine." Cora nodded. She had been through many things in her life, she knew she needed to stay strong. "Kent seemed like such a nice, young man. Who would ever do something like this to him?"

"Do what to him?" Penny stepped up beside them. "What do you mean? No one did anything to him."

"I beg to differ." Cora crossed her arms. "Clearly, he's been murdered."

"Murdered?" Penny broke out in a shocked laugh. "Clearly, he slipped down the ridge into the ditch and hit his head." She gestured to the sneakers on Kent's feet. "He must not have been paying attention during his run."

"Nonsense," Cora huffed. "I do believe you've made a mistake to assume something like that."

"It makes more sense to assume murder?" Penny narrowed her eyes. "I think perhaps you have been reading too many murder mysteries."

"Excuse me?" Cora's shoulders straightened.

"All right, the police are here." Samantha moved between them. "I'm sure that they'll sort all of this out. Emotions are certainly running high right now. Let's all just take a breath."

Cora took an exaggerated breath. "It doesn't

matter how much I breathe, it's still not going to change the fact that he was murdered!"

CHAPTER 6

"*L*et's give them a little space." Samantha steered Cora away from the shocked expressions of the people who surrounded Kent's body.

"Are you going to dismiss this, too?" Cora stared into her eyes. "Are you going to tell me that this looks like an accident to you?"

"I can't say what exactly it looks like." Samantha frowned. "But I agree, it's quite suspicious. You can't force anyone else to feel the same way, though."

"I'm not worried about forcing anyone else. I just want to be sure that the police are going to do their jobs." Cora sighed as she spotted a man in a suit headed in their direction. "Finally!" She flagged him over. "Detective, I assume? I do hope that you're taking this seriously!"

"I take any loss of life very seriously, ma'am. I'm

Detective Ian Greg." He flashed his badge before he pulled a notepad out of his back pocket. "Can you tell me anything about what happened here?"

"When Kent came up missing, I knew that something had to be terribly wrong." Cora shook her head. "I was trying to find him."

"And you came upon the body?" The detective looked up from the notepad at the two women in front of him.

"Yes," Samantha began to explain, but Cora stepped in front of her.

"The poor man. Such a tragedy. When he wasn't at the resort this morning, when he was meant to be, I just knew in my heart that something was wrong." Cora shook her head. "I guess I didn't find him fast enough."

"I see." The detective jotted down a few words in his notepad. "And how long had you known Kent?"

"Oh, a day." Cora shrugged.

"A bit less than a day, really," Samantha added in.

"You just met him yesterday?" The detective raised his eyebrows.

"Yes. I won a raffle, and this lovely vacation was my prize. I arrived yesterday and met Kent." Cora looked over her shoulder at Samantha. "Samantha arrived around the same time."

"Yes, just before Mrs. Bing," Samantha explained.

"You didn't know him? You just came out looking

for him after you learned that he was missing?" The detective looked between them.

"Yes, I just knew something was wrong. Apparently, it's not like him to be late to work, and the staff at the resort were panicking." Cora pursed her lips. "I had to do something. I couldn't just sit around."

"And you? What are you doing in Junction?" The detective turned his attention on Samantha.

"I'm just on vacation for a few days." Samantha didn't want the fact she was reviewing the resort revealed to prying ears. It's not like it would change things, anyway. "I came out here with Cora because I wanted to make sure that she was safe while she searched for him. We're both new to the area, and I was worried she might get lost." She winced as Cora huffed beside her.

"And you two have been friends for how long?" The detective's pen hovered over his notepad.

"A little less than a day," Samantha explained. "We only met yesterday."

"I need to know if you noticed anything along the trail, anything that might have frightened or distracted Kent. Anything that he might have tripped on or stumbled over." Detective Greg tapped his pen on his notepad.

"Tripped?" Cora narrowed her eyes.

"Stumbled?" Samantha repeated the word.

"We're trying to determine what might have

caused him to fall." Detective Greg lowered his notepad as both women zeroed in on him.

"Fall?" Cora shook her head. "He didn't just fall to cause those wounds. This was obviously murder."

Samantha nodded in agreement. She had seen quite a bit during her investigative journalist days, and from what she knew, falls didn't cause head wounds like that, especially seeing as the ridge wasn't that high, and there was nowhere to hit his head.

"We'll let the medical examiner determine that." Detective Greg quirked an eyebrow. "Do you have any evidence this was murder?"

"Common sense?" Cora frowned. "Clearly, he was struck by something. You can't be so incompetent not to realize that."

"Look, if you don't answer my questions properly, you're not going to be much help in determining what happened here." Detective Greg's tone hardened.

"We're not?" Cora laughed. "It seems to me that you are the one botching this whole investigation up! You should be looking for a murderer, not a tree root."

"Ma'am, you're going to have to settle down." Detective Greg took a slight step back.

"I will settle down when you do your job and find out what really happened to Kent!" Cora crossed her arms, her voice as sharp as the rocks that jutted out from the mountain.

"I will do my best." Detective Greg narrowed his eyes. "If you think of anything else that might be important, please call me." He handed them each a card, then turned, and walked over to Kent's body. Other officers now surrounded the body, all of the staff members of the resort had been shooed away.

"Oh, poor Kent." Cora pressed her hand against her chest.

"Let's get you back to your room, Mrs. Bing." Samantha gently took her by the arm and led her back up to the path. With each step she took, she wondered if Cora was overreacting, or simply very right. Kent had been murdered, and the police wouldn't do enough to get to the truth.

CHAPTER 7

Cora turned to look at Samantha as they walked down the trail.

"I can't believe Kent's dead."

"Me neither." Samantha nodded. "I've documented many things during my time as an investigative journalist, but some things still always shock me."

"An investigative journalist, you said?" Cora eyed Samantha for a moment.

"Yes, before I retired. It was challenging, but I really loved it." Samantha led her along the path back toward the lodge.

"You must have quite a lot of experience with crimes, then." Cora narrowed her eyes. "You probably could easily see that this was no accident."

"I suspect it wasn't, but until we have some proof of that, we can't say for sure that it wasn't." Samantha shrugged. "Maybe it's possible that he hit his head on the rocks near the water somehow."

"Really?" Cora huffed, then shook her head. "You and I both know that those rocks were too far away for him to have hit his head on."

"Maybe so, but we can't rule out the possibility that something very strange happened." Samantha held up her hands. "At least not until we find some kind of evidence that proves otherwise."

Samantha wished that her friend Eddy Edwards was there. He was a retired detective, and she was sure he would be able to help make sense of the scene and whether it could have possibly been an accident.

"Now, you sound like the police." Cora rolled her eyes. "Never mind, I'll figure this out on my own."

"Mrs. Bing, please. I'm not saying that I disagree with you. I just think that you should consider all the possibilities, until we find out more." Samantha paused outside the door of her room. "Maybe we could talk about it a bit more. We could compare notes and see if there's anything solid we can come up with to convince the police that this was a murder."

Cora narrowed her eyes as she stared at Samantha. Could Samantha have somehow been involved in Kent's murder? She knew from her mystery shows that everybody should be a suspect. Is that why Samantha hadn't wanted Cora to go after Kent? Because she had been the one to kill him? Samantha didn't strike her as a murderer, but then murderers rarely advertised their crimes.

"I'll figure this out on my own, thank you very much." Cora walked across the hall to her own room. As she turned back to close the door, she caught sight of Samantha still staring at her.

Cora pushed the door shut. Samantha had been a little bit too friendly. She'd tried to talk her out of going to look for Kent. She'd insisted on going with her, when she did go out to find him, and perhaps had intentionally slowed her down.

Had she engaged in small talk with Kent's future murderer? She paced back and forth the length of the room.

"If she was involved, then she must have gone out early enough to find him on his run." Cora recalled that Samantha was in the lobby with her book when the news of Kent being missing had broken. Why had Samantha been up so early on her first day of vacation? She could have slept in. She also could have read her book in her own room. Instead, she'd made it a point to be seen by others, maybe trying to create some kind of alibi or cover for herself.

Cora shook her head as she sat down on the edge of the bed again. Had she really been so blind to Samantha's true intentions? The day before, she thought she'd made a friend. When Samantha insisted that she would accompany her to look for Kent, she honestly thought the woman was quite kind, if not a bit overbearing. But maybe she had wanted to make sure that Cora didn't find something that would implicate Samantha as the killer.

Cora closed her eyes and tried to recall every detail of their walk along the trail. Samantha had stopped to catch her breath before they even stepped onto the path. She'd dismissed the shoe prints that Cora pointed out when she found them. Was it because the other shoe print belonged to Samantha? Her mind raced at the thought. There was only one way to find out. She'd have to get a measurement of Samantha's shoe to compare with the size of the print she'd seen on the path. She knew that it was smaller than Kent's, but it hadn't struck her as small enough to belong to a woman. Did Samantha have particularly large feet? She couldn't recall ever looking at the woman's shoes.

"Samantha, if it was you, I'm going to find out!" Cora stood and walked straight toward the door.

Before she could reach it, her cell phone rang. She pulled it out of her pocket with the intention of silencing the ring, but when she saw who it was from, she hesitated. Maybe it would be better to run her theory past someone she trusted before she demanded to see one of Samantha's shoes. She pressed the button to answer the phone and plopped back down on the edge of her bed.

"You will not believe what happened!" Cora sighed heavily into the phone.

CHAPTER 8

Samantha settled into the chair in front of the small desk near the only window in her room. She slid her laptop in front of her and opened it up. As a researcher by nature, she knew that the first thing she needed to do was find out as much as she could about Kent. She knew little more than his name. She'd heard Lincoln mention his full name to the police. Kent Walkers. Although Samantha still wondered if Kent's death might have been some kind of freak accident, she suspected that it was the result of murder. If that were the case, then someone had to have something against him, barring the slim possibility that a stranger had simply decided to end his life.

"Everyone has secrets." She stretched her fingers, then began typing on the keyboard.

After a few tries, she managed to narrow her

search down to the right Kent Walkers. Although he had a social media presence, he didn't post very often. She did find some pictures of the running trail, and the mountains.

She remembered the two sets of shoe prints on the trail. Was Kent running with someone? No one was with him when he was found.

She searched on Kent's social media pages for a possible running partner.

Samantha quickly found that he ran with someone named Nate Reed. She sifted through the numerous pictures that Nate had posted. Many of them featured Kent at his side as they started a new running trail. However, there were no posts from today. She also noticed that Kent didn't have too many friends. Those that he did have, didn't post very often to him. She guessed they weren't much more than acquaintances.

Samantha also noticed that prior to arriving at the lodge, Kent didn't have much presence online. As she skimmed through some of his information, she searched for any hint of a romantic partner. Aside from a few friends in a running group, she didn't find very many comments from females on any of his posts.

She shifted gears and began to dig into his career. He listed his previous employment as a hotel manager in the town of Bakersfield. He'd moved quite a distance to take his current job. She sat back in her chair and considered the possibilities of why. She doubted that the resort had made such a tantalizing offer that he'd decided to upend his entire life. Usually people moved because they wanted a fresh start, often because they wanted to leave something behind them. What did Kent want to leave behind?

She searched through local Bakersfield posts for his name. As she scrolled through, she noticed that he hadn't made one in years. As she skimmed through a few posts about local events and damaged trash cans, she realized she might have hit a dead end. If she had trouble finding out information about Kent's past, then she guessed the next best thing she could do was find out what she could about the last few months of his life.

Samantha stepped out through the door of her room and headed to the lobby. She noticed Penny talking to Detective Greg near the front desk.

Samantha hung back and listened in on the conversation as it unfolded.

"I just don't understand why you need this information, if it was an accident." Penny crossed her arms.

"Ma'am, we're just covering all of our bases at this point. It will be the medical examiner that determines the cause of death, not me. But it's always best to get as much information as possible right after an incident, while people's minds are still fresh. I just need to know where you were this morning." Detective Greg tapped his pen against the pad he held in his hand.

"Fine, I guess." Penny pursed her lips. "But I

really do think that your time could be spent in better ways."

"You may be right, but arguing about it is only wasting more time." The detective smiled, then tapped his pad again.

"Yes, true. I was here all morning, as were my brothers. Now, you won't have to waste your time asking them." Penny sighed as the dog she held by the collar began to tug at her grasp.

"You're sure about that?" The detective frowned. "None of you left the lodge at all this morning?"

"Yes, of course, I'm sure. We were all busy trying to contact Kent when he didn't arrive for work. He's very prompt, normally. We only left when we went searching for him." Penny looked down at Boomer. "Calm down, boy."

"And you said he lived here? He had a room here?" Detective Greg met her eyes.

"Yes, most of our staff live here. It's a perk of the job." Penny shrugged.

"And he'd been a reliable employee?" The detective glanced in Samantha's direction at the same moment that Boomer broke free of Penny's grasp.

Samantha gasped as he bolted straight for her. Only then did she realize that the dog had been trying to get to her the whole time.

"Hi, boy!" She laughed as he jumped up and placed his paws against her stomach. "It's good to see you, too."

"Boomer, down!" Penny marched over and grabbed the dog by the collar, again. "Detective, please, as you can see I'm very busy. Are we done here?"

"Yes, at least for the moment." The detective nodded to Penny, then to Samantha.

Samantha brushed some mud from her shirt and grinned at the dog, who she noticed was quite wet. He had obviously been for a swim.

"I guess he was eager to say hello."

"Yes, or maybe he wanted to know why you were lurking and eavesdropping." Penny raised her eyebrows. "Don't think I don't know who you are or why you're here." She lowered her voice. "It would be completely unfair to give a bad review for a tragedy that we couldn't possibly have prevented."

"Penny, don't worry about that." Samantha shook her head. "Of course, I know that none of this was your fault. My review is strictly about the resort itself, not what happened today."

"Well, that's a relief to hear." Penny sighed. "Now, if only the police would get to the bottom of this, our business might be able to survive."

"I'm sure they'll figure it out soon." Samantha frowned as she watched the other woman walk away.

Eager to avoid the detective, and to find out more information about Kent, Samantha sought out people she thought might have had a close relationship with him.

CHAPTER 9

Cora recounted as much of the story as she could to her friends gathered on a conference call back in Blue River.

"What a terrible thing to happen on your vacation." Betty sighed.

Betty had been one of Cora's closest friends since high school.

"Yes, it's terrible, but that's not the point. The point is that the police aren't doing their job! At least back home, the police would be on top of this, no question. Luke would find the killer in no time." Cora knew that Detective Luke Elm would have this solved quickly, especially with a little help from her and her friends.

"You don't know for sure that there is a killer," Pearl spoke up. "You're getting ahead of yourself, Mrs. Bing."

Pearl always thought she knew everything.

Unfortunately, most of the time she was right. But not this time.

"I'm telling you, this was no accident." Cora sighed into the phone. "If you were here, you would say the same thing."

"Would we?" Betty clucked her tongue. "I'm not sure that's the case. I think maybe you just have yourself worked up over all of this. I knew you shouldn't have gone off on your own."

"I'm fine on my own, thank you very much!" Cora frowned. "You're just not listening to me, as usual. Even Samantha agrees, a fall like that wouldn't cause the head wound that he had. You can't tell me any different!"

"We wouldn't even try," Betty laughed. "Once you're convinced of something, there's no changing your mind."

"That's because I'm right. You're both wrong, it wasn't an accident!" Cora clucked her tongue. "Now, I have to figure out who would do this to him. I can't let his killer just go free."

"Stop it," Pearl gasped. "You can't get yourself tangled up in all of this."

"Mrs. White is right," Betty chimed in. "You don't have us to back you up."

"Let alone Ally and Charlotte. They might run the chocolate shop, but they have a knack for solving murders." Pearl smiled at the thought of their sleuthing adventures.

"It simply isn't safe. You must come home at once." Betty's voice became stern.

"I am perfectly capable of investigating this on my own." Cora ended the call before her two closest friends could argue with her any further. "I'm not going home until I find out the truth."

Cora stepped out into the hallway. If she wanted to find the truth, she would have to start somewhere.

As she started in the direction of the lobby, she caught sight of a woman farther down the hall. It only took her a second to recognize Samantha, and another second to see that she was far past the entrance to her room. So, where was she headed?

The hairs on the back of Cora's neck stood up. She had already thought that Samantha was acting suspicious. Now she was sneaking around, and Cora intended to find out why.

As Cora trailed behind Samantha, she spotted a sign that pointed in the direction of the staff wing. Her heart skipped a beat as she realized that Samantha might be on her way to Kent's room. But why?

As Cora tried to come up with a reason for Samantha's behavior, nothing satisfied her. She liked the woman, but it sure looked like she was up to something that she shouldn't be. If she was responsible for Kent's death, then she would have to pay the price for it.

Cora flattened herself against the wall as Samantha glanced back over her shoulder. Cora held her breath as she wondered if she'd been spotted. She could hear Pearl's voice in her mind, chastising her about her paranoia. She would often tell her, "If only you would have a little more faith in people, you'd have more friends."

Cora rolled her eyes at the thought. She loved her two best friends, but neither of them had an ounce of sense. Pearl wanted everything proven to her, and Betty only ever heard what she wanted to hear.

It's important to think positive, my dear, Cora could hear Betty say, even though the hallway was silent. As much as she valued their friendship, she doubted their ability to spot a criminal without her.

Cora noticed Samantha pause in front of one of the doors. Cora ducked behind a large fern at the corner of the hallway and hoped its fronds would be broad enough to conceal her presence.

After a few seconds, Cora poked her head out. A bundle of flowers leaned beside the door. She presumed that someone wanted to honor Kent's memory, and this was his room. She watched as Samantha slid a key into the door. Her heart pounded as she watched the woman's hand curve around the door handle. What did she think she was doing? Where had she gotten the key? Had he given it to her? Maybe they had some sort of history she didn't know about.

No, she didn't think so.

Samantha broke out into a light sweat as she stood

outside Kent's room with the key in the door and her hand on the handle. She knew that if she was caught, she'd probably get thrown out of the lodge. She didn't want to lose her first paying job in so long, but she also had to do what she could to find out more about Kent's murder.

She had only intended to talk to the housekeeper to find out where Kent's room was, but when the housekeeper had placed her key in her cart as she went inside a room, Samantha managed to grab it.

Samantha's heart pounded as she looked up and down the hallway for any sign of people nearby. The leaves of the tall fern in the corner rustled when the air-conditioner turned on, but other than that, there was no movement. She turned the key in the door and hoped that it would open. The moment it did, she stepped inside and closed the door behind her.

Cora crept forward as Samantha stepped through the door. Just before the door could swing shut, she pressed her fingertips against the painted wood to prevent it from closing all the way.

Cora could call the police. She could summon an employee of the resort. But she knew that neither would get there in time. Samantha would take off before she could be caught. She couldn't let her get away with it. She held her breath and pushed the door open enough to see through it.

A few magazines were stacked on a table near the bathroom, along with a travel-size hair dryer. She noticed a potted plant on one shelf. And there was Samantha looking around Kent's room. She tried to decide what she should do next. If Samantha was the killer, what would she do to her when she noticed her presence?

Samantha took a deep breath and braced herself inside Kent's room. If anyone spotted her, she guessed they would be pounding on the door any second. As those seconds passed, she began to feel a bit braver. She stepped farther into the room and used her phone's flashlight to guide her. She guessed that turning on the light in the room might draw the wrong kind of attention.

Kent's room was neat, but as would be expected when living in a small space, there were a few piles of papers, clothes, and dishes around. She went straight for the papers. As she glanced over them, she noticed that they were all business related, with no personal notes. She left the stack on the table and walked over to the small kitchenette. In the trash can, near the sink, she noticed a few crumpled-up papers. A stray one lay beside the trash can. She presumed that Kent had missed when he threw the paper away. She picked up the paper and began to unfold it. Her eyes settled on a set of numbers and a name. As she straightened back up, she felt something solid and round push hard into her back.

"Don't you move a muscle!" a deep, gravelly voice demanded from just behind her.

Samantha's heart pounded as she wondered who might be behind her. Was it Kent's killer?

"Please," Samantha's voice wavered some. "Please don't hurt me." Her muscles tensed. At a moment like this, she would normally count on one of her friends back home in Sage Gardens showing up and saving her. But they wouldn't be doing that. No one would.

CHAPTER 10

"This is a citizen's arrest!" Cora cleared her throat as her voice cracked. It was far more difficult to make her voice deep than she thought.

"Cora?" Samantha spun around to face her, her eyes wide. "Is that a hair dryer?" She looked down at her hands.

"Uh, yes." Cora held it up. "Don't try anything funny. I've already called the police! I'm sure that they will be very interested to know just what you're doing in Kent's room. Did you come here to cover your tracks?"

"Cover my tracks?" Samantha looked past her at the slightly open door. "You called the police? Why would you do that?"

"Why do you think?" Cora glared at her. "Because you killed Kent! I should have known it when you tried to stop me from looking for him. You didn't want me to find him in time to save him."

"What?" Samantha took a step back as she stared at her. "Are you nuts? Of course I didn't kill Kent!"

"If you didn't kill Kent, where were you when he was killed?" Cora stepped in front of her.

"I was here at the lodge, reading my book in the lobby." Samantha shrugged. "You saw me in there, when you came out of your room."

"I saw you there, then, yes, but you can't prove you were there when Kent was killed." Cora moved again to block Samantha from exiting the room. "I'm not going to let you get away with this."

"Get away with what?" Samantha frowned. "I didn't kill anyone. You're the one that was flirting with the poor man. Forty years your junior, at least, and you were flirting with him like you were back in high school."

"Well, I never." Cora's cheeks flushed with a mixture of anger and embarrassment. "Don't you forget, I went out looking for him."

"That's a perfect way to cover up for a murder. To act as if you're concerned about the well-being of your victim. You wanted to throw everyone off, right?" Samantha stared into Cora's eyes. "Honestly, you don't strike me as a killer. But maybe you were up on that ridge together, and he said something hurtful. Maybe you just lost it?"

"Nonsense!" Cora glared at her. "I would never kill anyone!"

Voices from the hall silenced them both.

"We're going to search the room. Rope off the area, make sure no one goes in or out," the detective's voice carried through the door.

"Oh no." Cora gasped.

"Oh no, what?" Samantha narrowed her eyes. "You said you called the police, and now you're surprised they're here?"

"I didn't actually call the police." Cora winced as she backed away from the door. "I saw you walking in here, and I wanted to see what you were up to. I just told you that to make sure that you wouldn't kill me."

"Kill you?" Samantha huffed, then gasped as the footsteps drew closer. "We have to get out of here. If they catch us in here, we'll both be in handcuffs."

"How?" Cora groaned. "There's no way out!"

"The window." Samantha walked over to it and slid it open. She popped out the screen and looked down through it. "It's not too far down, we can make it."

"Are you crazy? I can't climb through the window!" Cora pointed to her pantyhose.

"Mrs. Bing! It's now or never!" Samantha gestured to the open window. "Hurry, I'll help you out."

Cora stared at her for a moment. She wasn't sure if Samantha was planning to kill her, or if she really did want to help her. Either way, she needed to get out of the room before the police caught her in there. She had done more daring things than jump out of an open window back in Blue River. But in Blue River she had the backup of her friends.

"All right." Cora forced a breath through her pursed lips, then swung her leg over the windowpane.

Samantha held tightly to her arm as she managed to swing the other leg over, then jump down.

Cora turned back just in time to see Samantha launching herself out through the window. She stepped closer in an attempt to catch her, but instead Samantha slammed into her and knocked them both to the ground.

"Ugh, I knew it!" Cora gasped as she wriggled underneath the larger woman. "You're trying to kill me!"

"I'm doing no such thing!" Samantha got to her feet. She grabbed Cora's hand and pulled her up off the ground. "Quiet, before they hear us out here!"

"Run!" Cora pushed her forward as the light in Kent's room snapped on.

CHAPTER 11

Samantha's heart raced as she hurried around the side of the lodge. She could hear Cora's footsteps right behind her. Despite her choice in footwear, she could move quite quickly. As she reached the front of the building, police lights flashed in all directions. Her stomach twisted, as for just a second she expected that they were there for her. Had the police officers spotted the two of them climbing out the window?

Cora slammed into her back, mumbled, then caught herself on Samantha's arm. "What are you doing? Why did you stop so suddenly?"

"Look." Samantha pointed to the circular driveway full of police cars.

"It seems they've finally caught on." Cora stepped up beside her. "Let's see what we can find out." She led the way into the lobby.

Samantha spotted Penny right away. She stood with her arms crossed, her gaze focused on the detective who spoke to her. Police officers spoke to guests and staff members in various areas of the lobby.

"Excuse me?" Samantha caught a staff member by the arm as he walked past. "Any idea what all of this is about?"

"Oh, yes." He glanced toward Penny, then turned back in Samantha's direction, and lowered his voice. "It turns out that accident that Kent had, wasn't an accident at all. The police now consider it a homicide. They're questioning everyone."

"Wow." Samantha did her best to look surprised as the man walked away.

"It's about time." Cora shook her head. "I thought they would never figure it out."

"Maybe we can find out some details from the detective." Samantha walked toward him.

"Oh no." Detective Greg took a step back. "Thanks, ladies, but I already have enough information from both of you."

"Oh, but we want to ask a question." Samantha smiled as the detective continued to back away.

"Officer Smith will answer your questions." The detective pushed a stunned officer toward them, then hurried off in the opposite direction.

"I think we must have made quite an impression." Cora grinned, then focused on the officer in front of her. "So? What's the story?"

"Story?" He shifted uncomfortably as he looked between them. "I'm not sure what you mean."

"I mean, we already know that he was murdered. But any idea how?" Cora raised her eyebrows.

"Oh, well, uh..." The officer glanced toward the detective.

"Just answer us. Trust me, he's not going to be happy, if we go ask him instead." Samantha settled her gaze on the officer. "All we want to know is what the medical examiner said."

"He said it looks like Kent was hit with something large, then shoved down the ridge and into the ditch." The officer frowned. "But I'm not sure I'm supposed to be telling you this."

"Never mind that." Cora waved her hand.

The officer looked up as the detective called his name. "I really have to find out what he needs."

"Of course." Samantha smiled. "Thank you for your help."

"You're very welcome." He turned and rushed over to the detective.

"Interesting." Samantha considered the officer's words. "So, clearly someone had to be close to Kent to strike him with something."

"Were you?" Cora locked her eyes with Samantha's. "How close, exactly? What did you use? A big, thick branch? A pipe of some kind?"

"Oh, would you stop!" Samantha huffed. "I had

nothing to do with Kent's death, and I think that you know that. Don't you?"

Cora's lips tightened, then she sighed.

"Okay, I guess I do. But until I can prove otherwise, you're still on my suspect list."

"Good, because you're still on mine." Samantha rolled her eyes. "But maybe we could spend our time trying to find the real killer, instead of wasting it on suspecting each other?"

"That seems fair." Cora held out her hand to her. "A team?"

"A team." Samantha shook it, then surveyed the lobby again. As her eyes settled on an officer interviewing the chef, Billy, she recalled the argument she'd overheard between him and Kent. "I think I just found our new prime suspect." She pointed the chef out to Cora. "He was quite upset with Kent, yesterday. So angry, in fact, that I can believe he might have wanted to hurt Kent." She relayed the details of the fight she'd overheard.

"Interesting." Cora frowned. "But we can't interrupt his interview. We'll have to come up with something else to start with. Any other ideas?"

"Actually, yes." Samantha dug into the pocket of her jeans. "I found this slip of paper beside the trash can in Kent's room." She met Cora's eyes. "Right before you shoved a hair dryer into my back."

"I had to use the tools available to me." Cora peered at Samantha's hand. "What's on the paper?"

"A woman's name, and phone number." Samantha spread the paper out. "It could mean anything. But when I looked into Kent, he didn't seem to have a girlfriend, and only a couple of female friends, for that matter. I didn't come across anyone with this name. Anne. So, maybe it was someone new he met? If it was, then she might have some idea of what was going on recently in his life."

"I didn't realize you already looked into Kent." Cora smiled some as she looked up from the paper. "You really are an investigator, aren't you?"

"It's my passion." Samantha started to fold up the piece of paper. "I guess we'll have to contact her, if we want to know more."

"Well then, what are we waiting for?" Cora snatched the paper out of Samantha's hand and, at the same moment, pulled her phone out of her purse.

"Mrs. Bing, wait! We should figure out what we're going to say first." Samantha sighed as she saw the other woman was already dialing the number.

"I always do my best work when I wing it." Cora winked at her. "Besides, how hard can it be to find out why someone murdered someone? I'll start by asking."

"Please, don't ask her that!" Samantha winced.

CHAPTER 12

As the phone began to ring in her ear, Cora tried to swat Samantha's hand away from grabbing at it.

"Stop, it's ringing."

"Please, hang up, please." Samantha dodged the swat and managed to grab the bottom of Cora's phone. "Think about what you're doing, Mrs. Bing."

"Oh, now you've done it," Cora grumbled as she lowered the phone. "You made me hang up before it could even get to the second ring."

"Good. Listen. What if Anne turns out to be a family member or close friend, and we're the first people to inform her that Kent died?" Samantha placed her hands on her hips as she stared at her. "That's not something that should be taken lightly."

"You're right." Cora sighed. "It's not." Then she narrowed her eyes. "But if Anne was someone he was close to, then why would he have to write her phone number down? Most people know the phone numbers of their loved ones, right?"

"Maybe. But these days phone numbers just get stored in a phone. Maybe he got a new phone and jotted the number down until he could enter it into the new phone." Samantha shrugged. "But that's not the point. The point is we need to figure out what we're going to say before you start asking questions. If this woman is somehow involved in Kent's death, then we will only have one shot at taking her by surprise. If we mess that up, then we might never find out the truth."

"And you're just assuming I would mess it up?" Cora gazed at Samantha as her lips curled up with distaste. "Why? Because I'm older than you?"

"Because you're impulsive, and unpredictable!" Samantha threw her hands in the air. "In the short time I've known you, you've led me to a dead body and held me hostage with a hair dryer!"

"I do what I have to do." Cora took a slight step back. "If you can't see the value in that, then maybe we shouldn't be working together."

"Mrs. Bing." Samantha sighed. "Our emotions are running high. Let's just see if we can make a plan, okay? Can we at least have an idea of who you're going to say you are when you call?"

"I'll say I'm doing a survey. I'll ask some general questions, and see if I can get some information from her. Is that vague enough?" Cora did her best to calm down, as she realized that Samantha did want to help.

"It's a good start. Let's see how far it gets us." Samantha gestured toward Cora's phone. "Go ahead, give her a call."

"Okay, here we go." Cora dialed the number, then held her breath. As the phone began to ring, she looked around the lobby at the others gathered there. Any one of them might have some small speck of information that could lead to the truth about Kent's death. The murderer needed to be found.

Cora frowned as the phone continued to ring.

"No answer?" Samantha wiped her palms on her jeans.

"Nothing yet." Cora noticed that the phone ringing in her ear seemed to correlate with another ring. One a few feet away from her. "That's odd."

"What's odd?" Samantha met her eyes.

"Every time I hear the ring in my phone, I also hear a ring coming from that woman's back pocket. What are the chances that the rings could be timed so perfectly?" Cora narrowed her eyes as a generic voicemail greeting picked up.

"That's a good question." Samantha looked over at the woman whose phone stopped ringing at that moment. "She looks a bit familiar to me. Maybe she's a guest here. I'm guessing it could be her phone number. What do you think?"

"There's one way to find out." Cora dialed Anne's

number again. As soon as she heard the second ring in her ear, the phone belonging to the woman who stood a few feet away, began to ring as well. Still not convinced, Cora let it ring twice, then abruptly hung up. The moment she hung up, the woman's phone silenced as well.

"That's it." Samantha nodded. "It's got to be her. I remember her now. I saw her in the lobby, in the sitting area, when I checked in. I noticed she was pretending to read a book, but she was staring at Kent. I presumed she fancied him. She's been here longer than we have."

"Then it sounds like she's someone that we need to talk to." Cora began to walk in her direction.

"Wait, Mrs. Bing." Samantha caught her by the arm. "Just take a breath. Let's keep an eye on her and see if we can confirm who she is before we confront her." She searched her eyes as Cora pulled her arm away. "Don't you want to do this the right way? We have to be cautious."

"Cautious?" Cora stared back at her. "There isn't time to be cautious, my dear. Kent is dead, and every minute that his killer is free, is a minute more that he or she has to escape the police entirely. Yes, the detective will be held back by red tape and required procedures, but we're just average citizens acting on our curious natures. Nothing to hold us back. So, no, I don't think we should be cautious."

"At least give me a second to think of a good cover

story to find out if she is Anne and how she knew Kent." Samantha sighed, her expression tight, and her shoulders even more tense.

Cora suspected Samantha had some control issues. But she wasn't one to let other people's hang-ups slow her down.

"Sure, you think about it." Cora gave Samantha a quick smile, then turned around to face the woman she suspected was Anne. Either she had something to do with Kent's death, or she knew something about Kent that might be relevant, and they needed to find it out. There wasn't a single second to waste. Before she decided to do it, Cora's hand was in the air as she walked toward the woman. "Anne? Oh, Anne, is that you?"

Cora heard Samantha gasp from just behind her.

CHAPTER 13

Samantha's heart slammed against her chest as she tried to catch up with what Cora had just done. Not only had the woman completely ignored her warning, but she'd gone with her own plan that could ruin any chance they had of finding out if the other woman was indeed Anne.

The woman turned around to look at Cora. At that moment, Cora stepped behind Samantha.

The woman stared at Samantha, her eyes narrowed, her expression tense, as she waited for an explanation.

Samantha's mind worked swiftly to recognize that the woman had responded to Cora calling her name, but now she believed that it was Samantha who had sought her attention. As she realized that this woman was indeed Anne and must be the same Anne whose name and number Kent had written down on a piece of paper, maybe not long before he died, she knew that she had to work quickly.

"Oh, Anne, don't you remember me?" Samantha's lips spread into a broad smile. "It's so good to see you again!"

"I'm sorry, I don't know who you are." Anne looked into her eyes, then frowned. "I just can't place you."

"Oh, it's all right. We met only once, and it was a long time ago." Samantha offered a soft laugh. "But I do remember you. I'm a friend of your father's." She offered her hand to Anne. "My name is Samantha. Your father and I worked together briefly."

"Oh." Anne smiled as she took Samantha's hand. "Sorry, I just don't remember."

"It's all right, don't worry about that. Life is so busy, I know how hard it can be to keep track of everything." Samantha took a deep breath, then sighed as she looked around the crowded lobby. "With all of this going on, it's just nice to see a familiar face in the crowd."

"This is wild, isn't it?" Anne crossed her arms as she surveyed the room. "I never expected to be involved in a police investigation."

"And he seemed like such a nice man." Samantha's voice softened as she glanced down at her feet. "I only met him once, but he seemed like a nice person."

"Did he?" Anne quirked an eyebrow as she studied her. "I suppose any loss is a great tragedy, isn't it?"

"It is, especially when it's unexpected, and he was so young." Samantha took a deep breath, then sighed again. "Did you know him well?"

"Me?" Anne shook her head as she glanced back at the police officers scattered throughout the room. "I didn't know him at all."

"You'd never met him?" Samantha's heart skipped a beat. The way that Kent had taken the time to greet her, and then Cora, when they arrived, made her think that he did that with all of the guests.

"Not that I know of or can recall." Anne shrugged as she looked back at Samantha. "I just arrived for a vacation, and I never expected anything like this to happen. I'm sure he was a very nice man, though. I do hope that the police find out what happened to him. It's such a shame." She closed her eyes for a moment. A ripple of what appeared to be pain creased her forehead and lips, then vanished as soon as it appeared. She opened her eyes again and managed a small smile. "I do hope that you're still able to enjoy some of your vacation, Samantha. I'll be sure to mention seeing you, to my father. I'm sure he'll be thrilled that we had the chance to reconnect." She turned to walk away.

"Great." Samantha stepped closer to her before she could get too far. "Maybe we'll see each other again before we leave?"

"Maybe." Anne smiled again, this time even tighter. "I think I may be leaving soon, though. All of this has taken all of the fun out of the vacation for me. It's hard to enjoy the scenery without thinking about someone being killed nearby. Don't you think?"

"I agree." Samantha nodded, then watched as Anne walked away. Her chest tightened with a sense of dread. Her instincts told her that she needed to stop Anne before she left the resort. If she left, she might run, and the police might not have a proper chance to investigate her. After the conversation they just had, she believed she absolutely needed to be investigated.

"Great job, Samantha." Cora stepped up beside her and crossed her arms as she stared after Anne.

"Great job?" Samantha looked over at Cora. "Is that all you have to say to me after that stunt you just pulled?"

"Stunt?" Cora blinked her eyes innocently. "What do you mean?"

"You know what I mean. You threw me under the bus. What if I hadn't been able to come up with anything? What if I had just blurted out some nonsense that made her walk away? What if the story I made up never rang true?" Samantha glared at her. "You really need to think before you act."

"Oh, Samantha, you shouldn't doubt yourself so much." Cora rolled her eyes. "I knew you'd do just fine. I have plenty of faith in you. And it turns out that I was absolutely right. You did fantastic. Everything turned out okay. Now we know all we needed to know about Anne."

"How do you figure that?" Samantha frowned, though she did feel a bit of warmth in response to Cora's compliment. "All we know is that she's Anne. That's not a lot to go on."

"Oh no, we know a lot more than that." Cora smiled as she looked into Samantha's eyes. "We know that she's Anne, and we also know that Anne is a liar."

Samantha's heart fluttered at the thought. Of course, she had to be a liar. Kent knew her name and her phone number. How could that be possible without knowing her.

"Maybe." She narrowed her eyes. "Or maybe, Kent's the liar." She winced as Cora's expression darkened. "Hear me out. What if Kent knew Anne, but Anne didn't know Kent?"

"You mean, he was stalking her?" Cora shook her head. "That would be terrible."

"It could explain why he had her name and phone number. Maybe he wasn't stalking her, but maybe there was a reason that he wanted to speak to her. He could have gotten her information from the computer after she checked in. I think it's a possibility, don't you?" Samantha met Cora's eyes.

"Yes." Cora sighed. "I suppose it is."

CHAPTER 14

Although Cora doubted Samantha's suspicions about Anne not knowing Kent, she couldn't completely dismiss them, either. Instead, she had to open her mind and consider that Kent could have been up to something nefarious. The thought sent a shiver down her spine.

"Well, we won't know anything more, if we don't start digging into this investigation, will we?" Cora frowned. "Standing around here isn't getting us anywhere."

"You're absolutely right." Samantha tilted her head toward Billy as he started to walk away from the lobby. "One of us should speak to Billy, the chef, while we have the chance. I'd like to dig more into Anne's past. If I catch up to her, I should be able to figure out which room she's in, then I can get the information I need to find out who she is. Do you want to talk with Billy?"

"Sure, I can do that." Cora's heart skipped a beat as she wondered if Billy had killed Kent. "Any tips?"

"Just be careful." Samantha pursed her lips. "He was very angry when I heard him arguing with Kent. He might be unpredictable. Don't push him too hard." She sighed. "You know what? Maybe I should be the one to talk to him."

"Nonsense!" Cora stepped in front of her. "I can handle this just fine. Besides, you're the one with all of the research know-how. You need to figure out how Anne connects to all of this."

"All right, but please, just don't antagonize him, okay?" Samantha looked into her eyes.

"Me, antagonize anyone?" Cora smiled. "I would never do such a thing." As she walked toward Billy, she wondered exactly how she would get more information out of him. If he had a conflict with Kent, then there was a very good chance that he had something to do with Kent's murder. But she couldn't come right out and say that, could she? He didn't really look like the friendly type.

As Cora followed him back toward the kitchen, she noticed that he moved quickly and shook his head repeatedly. It was clear that he was agitated. She certainly didn't want to make his agitation worse, or he would never talk to her. Instead, she had to approach things in a different way.

"Oh, oh my!" She gasped and lunged against the wall not far from Billy. She made sure her shoulder hit hard enough to create a loud thump that he would be certain to notice.

"What's wrong?" Billy spun around to face her, his eyes wide.

Cora draped her hand across her forehead as she continued to lean against the wall.

"Oh dear, in all of this excitement, I haven't had a bite to eat today. I have these spells, my doctor said it might be low blood sugar." Cora peeked past her hand at him. "I thought I could make it to the kitchen, but I'm just so dizzy."

"The kitchen is closed." Billy crossed his arms as he stared at her. His rugged features made him look older than she guessed he was. His well-worn shoes indicated that his paycheck wasn't very much. She guessed that he didn't have a lot of patience with seemingly wealthy guests making demands.

"I'm so very sorry. I guess I'll just try to make it back to my room. I think I have some crackers in there." Cora started to stand straight up, then immediately collapsed back against the wall. "Oh, if only the hallway would stop spinning!"

"All right, all right." Billy sighed and wrapped his long fingers around her arm. "Steady now. I'll get you some juice or something." He helped her down the hall toward the kitchen's entrance. "You should keep something with you, if you have low blood-sugar problems, you know?"

"I know, I know. I just always forget. Traveling alone makes it so hard. I have no one as kind as you to remind me." Cora settled into a chair he offered her. "Thank you so much."

"You're welcome." Billy poured her a glass of juice. "I didn't mean to be rude, it's just the owners asked me to close the kitchen while the police are investigating." He handed her the glass.

"Oh yes, this is perfect, thank you." Cora took a sip of the juice. "After what happened, I don't blame them. And look at me, I'm asking you for things when you're probably grieving your boss."

"He wasn't my boss," Billy snapped his words, then frowned. "Sorry."

"It's all right. Death brings out all kinds of emotions." Cora tilted her head to the side. "And I know that not everyone loves their boss."

"Just drink your juice. I have to make some calls." Billy pulled his phone out of his pocket, dialed a number, and put it to his ear.

Cora swirled her juice in her glass. She hadn't made much progress with getting him to tell her anything, but she hoped listening in to his phone conversation might tell her something.

"No. I said I wanted the first flight. I don't care what it costs. I've got a credit card. Just find me the flight." Billy ended the call.

"Going on vacation?" Cora smiled as he glanced back at her.

"No, I'm getting out of town." Billy stared at the glass in her hand. "I'm pretty sure it only works if you drink it."

"Oh, you're absolutely right." Cora laughed, then took another sip. "I'm surprised you want to leave in such a hurry. Last-minute flights can be very expensive. What has you on the run?" She winked at him. "You're not the killer, are you?"

"No!" Billy smacked his hand against the table hard enough to cause her elbow to jolt where it rested on the edge of the table.

"Sorry." Cora swallowed hard as she recalled Samantha's warning. "I was joking. I didn't mean to offend you."

"It's not you." Billy sighed. "It's the police. It's pretty well known around here that Kent and I didn't get along. So, the cops are all over me now. I don't have any money for a lawyer. They're going to lock me up, if I don't get out of here fast!"

"Oh, I see your concern." Cora's heart raced as she wondered if he really was the murderer. Why else would he want to leave so quickly? "But I'm sure the police will find the real killer. If you're innocent, you should have nothing to worry about."

"Wrong." Billy looked straight into her eyes. "When the police see a guy like me, with nothing, they think they can just run right over me. Once they have me in handcuffs, they'll stop looking for the truth." He looked back at his phone. "I have to make some more calls. Like I said, the kitchen is closed." He pointed to the door.

Cora decided not to argue with him. She doubted he would tell her anything more. She left her half-empty glass and headed for Samantha's room.

CHAPTER 15

Samantha wondered if she'd made the wrong choice by sending Cora off to talk to Billy. She'd seen how angry he was with Kent and worried that he might be just as angry with Cora. However, she doubted that she could talk the woman out of it, she definitely had a mind of her own.

As Samantha caught up with Anne, she noticed that the woman walked quickly, as if there was some urgency behind her movements. Samantha kept her distance and noticed that Anne glanced back over her shoulder several times. Was she nervous? As she turned down a hallway, she realized that Anne was headed to the staff wing.

Samantha hung back even farther. If Anne spotted her now, it would be obvious that she was following her. As she turned the corner, she spotted Anne down the hall, not far from Kent's room. The young woman froze at the sight of two officers who stood outside the room. She backed up, then turned around.

Samantha just managed to duck into the open door of a storage closet before Anne could spot her. Her heart raced as the woman hurried past her in the hallway. Clearly, she didn't want to interact with the police. Not that Samantha could blame her, it wasn't her favorite thing to do, either. But why had she gone to Kent's room? Cora had been right, Anne was definitely a liar. But why? Could she really be a killer?

Samantha waited a few moments, then stepped out of the closet, and followed Anne back through the winding corridors of the lodge.

When Anne finally stopped in front of a room and pulled a key out of her pocket, Samantha made a note in her mind of the room number. With that information, she could hopefully find out Anne's full name. She headed back to the lobby and found Penny at the front desk.

"Penny, how are you doing?" Samantha paused in front of the desk.

"It's a very trying day." Penny leaned against the counter, then sighed. "What can I help you with?"

"Oh, I had such a terrible moment today. I was so upset about this situation, and this young woman happened to be in my way at an inopportune time, and I was so very abrupt with her. I'd like to send her an apology note." Samantha shook her head. "But I don't know her name. I do have her room number. Do you think you could do me a favor and look her up for me? I just feel terrible, it's not normally how I behave at all."

"We're all stressed with all of this." Penny's voice tightened, and her eyes filled with tears. "Honestly, I know we didn't know him long, a little over a year, but he'd become like a younger brother to me."

"Better than the one you're stuck with, right?" A young man slouched against the side of the counter and settled his gaze on Penny.

"Don't talk like that, Collin." Penny looked at him. "Of course I'm happy with the brothers I have, but that doesn't mean I can't grieve for Kent. He was a good man."

"Sure he was." Collin narrowed his eyes, then glanced over at Samantha. "What's the room number? I can look it up for you." He walked around the side of the counter. "You should rest." He looked over at Penny. "I can handle this."

"Oh, thank you." Penny walked around the counter and headed for a chair in the lobby.

Samantha told Collin Anne's room number. "Thank you so much for your help. It must be hard to see your sister so upset." She glanced over at Penny.

"She gets upset about everything." Collin rolled his eyes. "Trust me. She'll be fine in a day or two." He tapped a few keys. "Her name is Anne Rodgers." He looked up at her. "Is that all you need?"

"I hope so. I feel so terrible for the way I behaved. Maybe I could order her something special and have it sent to her room? I know Kent said he would take care of anything I needed, but with him gone, can I still do something like that?"

"I can do it." Collin cleared his throat. "What would you like? Flowers? Wine?"

"Let me think about it, and I'll let you know." Samantha smiled at him. "Thanks again for your help."

As Samantha walked back to her room, she mulled over Collin's reaction in her mind. It seemed to her that he wanted to prove that he could do the job far better than Kent. Could his jealousy over Kent have driven him to commit murder? She recalled Penny telling the detective that she and her brothers had all been at the lodge all morning. That should eliminate him as a suspect. But it might be possible he left the lodge and Penny didn't know about it.

Samantha stepped into her room as she continued to consider the possibility. Without a doubt, she had to add Collin to the suspect list. But how likely was it that he had committed the crime? She quickly did a search on Collin. There wasn't much on his social media page. There were big gaps where there were no posts from him.

She pushed Collin from her mind as she turned her

focus on Anne. It didn't take long to match her name to a face on a social media profile.

As she skimmed through the content on the page, she came across a very familiar name. Bakersfield. The same town where Kent was from.

She saw a plea for information on a hit-and-run accident from a couple of years ago.

Anne, who was only in her early twenties, walked home from work each night along the same path she always took. She'd been struck by a hit-and-run driver. The police had no information about the driver, and the investigation had gone cold. Anne had spent many months in hospital. She was eventually released, but her hands had been injured. Her dreams of being a professional concert pianist had been dashed.

From the posts, it appeared that Anne had made it her mission to find out who had hit her. Who had taken her career away from her. It looked like she was obsessed with it.

Samantha's heart skipped a beat as she found a comment from Kent expressing his sympathies and anger at the accident. She recognized the connection between Kent and Anne. Which meant they likely knew each other well. Anne's vacation in Junction couldn't have been a coincidence, could it? She couldn't have just happened to have booked a room at the same place that Kent worked, could she? Samantha guessed that Anne had come there for a reason. She just needed to figure out what that reason was.

After a quick knock, Cora stepped through the door without waiting for an invitation. She threw her hands in the air and smiled. "Well, I've done it, Samantha. I've found the killer!"

CHAPTER 16

Cora beamed with pride as she dropped down into a chair beside Samantha.

"Well?" Samantha stared at her. "Did Billy confess?"

"Not exactly. But he might as well have. He's making plans to skip town." Cora crossed her arms as she sat back in her chair. "Which makes him guilty as sin, in my eyes."

"I think you might be getting ahead of yourself with that. Wait until you hear what I found out about Anne." Samantha turned her computer to face Cora.

"What's all this?" Cora squinted at the screen, which was populated with multiple windows.

"Anne and Kent are from the same hometown, where Anne was struck by a hit-and-run driver. She was a concert pianist, but the injuries to her hands from the accident mean she can never play properly again." Samantha pointed to the window that listed that information. "To this day, the driver hasn't been found. However, the timing correlates with Kent's move here. He moved here shortly after the accident, to take over as manager of the resort."

"Okay?" Cora frowned. "I still don't follow exactly what you're saying. Why does it matter if they're from the same hometown? I mean, other than Anne claiming not to know him."

"It matters because maybe Kent didn't apply for the job here, just for the opportunity. Maybe he needed to get away from Bakersfield, maybe because he'd been involved in something criminal, like a hit-and-run." Samantha raised her eyebrows as she released a slow breath.

"Now, who's getting ahead of themselves?" Cora sighed. "That is a huge conclusion to jump to. You think Kent was responsible for Anne's accident?"

"I think it's possible. I do know that we don't have enough information or evidence to support it. But it would explain Anne's presence here. Maybe she came here because she finally figured out who hit her, who killed her dreams, and she was ready to seek revenge. It would make sense, wouldn't it?" Samantha leaned forward in her chair. "Yes, we need some evidence to prove it, but I think the motive is there."

"The motive is there, if she really did believe that Kent hit her. But what if she just came here because Kent is her friend?" Cora looked over the information on the screen. "Maybe she wanted to get away, and he offered her a place to stay."

"Of course, that's possible, too, but if that were the case, why would she claim not to know Kent? I mean, they must have known each other. Kent commented on a post about her accident. He expressed his anger and sympathy." Samantha pointed at the screen. "Maybe he did that because he felt remorse for his actions."

"There's no question she's lying to us." Cora pursed her lips. "She knew Kent. But why is she lying to us? Is there any reason other than her being responsible for his death?"

"I'm not sure." Samantha tapped her fingertips lightly against her knee as she sat back in her chair. "I'm still considering the possibilities."

"While we consider the possibilities, there's a good chance that Billy's escaping. So, we need to do something about that before he has a chance to get too far." Cora pulled out her phone. "I think it's time we call the detective and let him know what we've found out."

"I think it may be too late for that." Samantha walked toward a window that overlooked the parking lot outside of the lodge. "It looks to me like the detective might have figured out the same information."

"What do you mean?" Cora followed her over to the window. She spotted a police car with flashing lights, and Billy in cuffs, being led to the car. "Oh dear, it looks like you're right. I wonder if he confessed to the detective?"

"I wonder if he's really the guilty party?" Samantha turned to face her. "During my time as an investigator, I came across instances where a suspect was innocent but was both arrested and convicted of a crime. I don't think we should just assume that the police have the right guy."

"I agree." Cora stared out through the thick glass as Billy was guided into the back seat of the police car. "We need to at least find out why Anne is really here. We know she's lying. Where there's a lie, there's a reason. While the police get to the bottom of things with Billy, we can find out more about him from his coworkers. I'll see if there are any kitchen staff that are close to Billy. I can try to find out what they know about Billy's relationship with Kent. If there's more to find out there, I'm sure that I'll discover it." She turned her focus back to Samantha. "Meanwhile, I think you know what you have to do to find out more about Anne."

"Make some calls to her family back home? And get in touch with the police officers that investigated the hit-and-run?" Samantha made a few notes on a piece of paper.

"No, that's not it at all." Cora sighed. "Do I have to spell it out for you?"

"Maybe?" Samantha narrowed her eyes as she studied Cora. "What are you talking about?"

"I'm talking about getting inside her room. We need to find out what she's hiding. Calling people back home isn't going to give us enough information. We need to know for sure, if she suspected Kent, and if she did, whether she was here to kill him. The only way we're going to find out that information is by getting into her room." Cora smiled.

"Are you suggesting I break in?" Samantha bit down on her bottom lip. "What if I get caught?"

"Don't act so innocent. You did break into Kent's room, you know?" Cora placed her hands on her hips. "Are you trying to pretend you had nothing to do with that?"

"That was different." Samantha frowned. "Kent's gone. Anne is just a suspect. And I had a key, which I placed back in the cart afterward. I didn't break in."

"I understand, dear. Would you rather I do it?" Cora offered her a sweet smile.

"What?" Samantha gasped, then rolled her eyes. "No! Definitely not." She looked straight into Cora's eyes. "Promise me you will not break into her room, or anyone's room, for that matter."

"Of course, I won't break in anywhere, as long as you're willing to do it." Cora shrugged.

"Fine!" Samantha ran her palm across her forehead and sighed. "Fine, I'll do it."

"Great." Cora winked at her, then stepped out into

the hallway. "I also might not be the best at picking locks."

"Me neither." Samantha cringed. "But I could give it a try. I've been learning from my friend Jo, back home. She's an expert."

"You're friends with an expert lock-picker?" Cora raised her eyebrows. "Why, exactly?"

"It's a long story." Samantha gave a short laugh.

CHAPTER 17

The thought of breaking into Anne's room made sweat form along the back of Samantha's neck. What if she was caught? The close call with the police in Kent's room had put her on edge. For the hundredth time since she'd come across Kent's body, she wished her friends from Sage Gardens were there with her. As she walked in the direction of Anne's room, she recalled the instructions that Jo had given her, more than once. Find the resistance, then back off, then break it.

Cora was right. Anne was hiding something, and she had to find out the truth. If that meant taking a few risks, then so be it.

Samantha neared Anne's room and noticed that her door was slightly open. Her heart skipped a beat as she wondered if she could have really gotten so lucky. Had Anne already checked out? Or had she accidently left her door open? Or was she inside? The possibility made the hairs on the back of her neck stand up. She stepped closer to the door and gave it a light push.

"Hello? Anne?"

"Yes?" A voice came from right behind her.

Samantha spun around to find Anne, with two suitcases in her hands. "Oh, Anne, hi."

"Hi." Anne set the suitcases down and looked straight into Samantha's eyes. "Are you here to make up more stories about how you know my dad?"

"Anne, I'm sorry about that." Samantha's muscles tensed as she prepared herself for Anne's anger. "I just wanted to know more about you."

"Clearly." Anne pointed toward her open door. "What exactly were you doing going into my room?"

"I thought you might be inside." Samantha cleared her throat. "Anne, I think it's time I come clean."

"Oh? Now, that you're caught?" Anne crossed her arms. "I can see why you might think it's time."

"Anne, listen." Samantha felt a rush of confidence as she squared her shoulders. "I know that you lied to me. I know that you knew Kent, and in fact, I think you knew him very well. If you don't want me sharing that information with the police, then you need to come clean."

"You know that, do you?" Anne picked up her suitcases and carried them with her through the door of her room. "Are you coming?" She looked back over her shoulder.

"Sure, yes I am." Samantha followed her, relieved that she hadn't simply shut the door in her face.

"Close it." Anne set her suitcases down beside her bed.

"I thought you might have left already." Samantha closed the door, then hovered close to it, aware that she might be alone in a room with a murderer.

"I was about to. A taxi was waiting for me. But when I headed for it, I couldn't get into it." Anne sank down on the edge of her bed. "I wanted to go, but I couldn't. Not without knowing what happened to Kent."

"Tell me the truth, Anne, why did you really come here?" Samantha sat down in a wooden chair and settled her gaze on her. "I'm listening."

"I came here because Kent asked me to." Anne narrowed her eyes. "He didn't explain why, just asked me to come. But I knew that it had to be something important. I knew that he wouldn't have called me otherwise. So, I came."

"And?" Samantha studied every twitch of the woman's face in an attempt to detect a lie.

"And, now he's dead. We never even had a chance to talk about whatever he wanted to talk about. I arrived, he greeted me, and assured me we would talk later. But we didn't." Anne sighed as she looked up at the ceiling. "I wish I had just made him talk to me. But of course, I had no idea what would happen."

"So, you didn't suspect him?" Samantha's voice softened.

"Suspect him of what?" Anne's eyes widened.

"Of having some involvement with your accident?" Samantha blurted out.

Anne stared at her, obviously stunned as her mouth hung half-open. "What do you know about that?"

"Just what I found out from social media and the articles about the accident." Samantha realized she might have pushed her too far, too fast. "Anne, I'm very sorry that this happened to you. I can't imagine what you went through, what you must still be going through. But I mean, it's quite a coincidence for you to be here and for him to be killed, right?"

"Are you asking me, if I had something to do with Kent's death?" Anne gasped. "Are you asking me, if I think that he hit me?"

"I'm not accusing you of anything, but I do want to know if you thought he was the hit-and-run driver." Samantha sensed the genuine shock in Anne's voice.

"Of course not." Anne stood up. "How could you even think such a thing? Kent was my friend. He helped me after the accident. He would never do anything to hurt me, and I would never do anything to hurt him. You have no reason to think that I would." She pointed to the door. "Please leave me alone."

"Wait, Anne, please." Samantha stood up. "You have to understand, I was only going with the information that I had at the time. I didn't know that the two of you were very close friends."

"Be honest. You thought that I might be a murderer." Anne narrowed her eyes. "Someone took my dreams from me. All I ever wanted to do was play the piano, and someone took that from me. Someone ran me down with their car, then didn't even bother to stop to try to help me. They ruined my life, and they wouldn't even stop to help me. I would never kill anyone. Do I want to find who hit me? Yes, of course I do. But I want to find who did this to me, so that person can face justice. I want them to suffer like they've made me suffer. If I kill them, they won't suffer. Death would be too easy for them. Now, please leave. I don't want to talk about this anymore."

Samantha opened her mouth to say more, but Anne pointed to the door, again.

Dejected, Samantha stepped through the door. She'd played her hand, and now all of her cards were on the table. Unfortunately, it hadn't given her much more information about Anne.

CHAPTER 18

Cora spotted a man in a kitchen uniform. He was just about to step out the front door of the lodge. Before he could, Lincoln shouted to him.

"Max! What are you doing? I was just in the kitchen, and I don't see anything prepped for tomorrow." He moved swiftly across the lobby with every intention of stopping the younger man.

"I've got to run an errand." Max turned to face him. "Don't worry, the prep will get done."

"I am worried, of course I am. Everything is in chaos right now, with Kent gone, and now Billy being questioned by the police. I need to know that the kitchen isn't in chaos as well. I need things to run smoothly. I need our guests to be taken care of, or none of us may have a job to come back to." Lincoln stared hard into Max's eyes. "Do you understand me?"

"Yes, sir, of course I do." Max stared back at him.

"I need to pick up a few groceries for the kitchen, that's all. I'll be back in no time."

"I happen to know that Billy already had a delivery today." Collin walked up to the two of them. "I saw him unloading it. So, I doubt there is anything you need to get at the grocery store. What are you really up to, Max?"

"Enough, Collin." Lincoln shot him a stern look. "Max and I will work this out."

"Lincoln, I'm the manager now." Collin narrowed his eyes. "I should be the one to handle this."

"No, Collin." Lincoln put his hand on Collin's shoulder. "That hasn't been decided. I know with Kent's death you might feel you are ready to step into that role, but Penny and I aren't sure you're ready for that kind of responsibility. Not after everything that's happened."

"I'm not ready?" Collin rolled his eyes. "Maybe if I had been in charge from the beginning, none of this would have happened." He turned his gaze on Max. "Get in that kitchen and prep for tomorrow, whatever you need to do can wait! It's that, or no paycheck, got it?"

Max shrank back from the two men. He appeared to be in his late teens or early twenties.

"Sure, okay, whatever you say." He held up his hands. "I'm just trying to do what everyone wants me to do. I'll get right on it." He stepped around Collin and headed for the kitchen.

"Unbelievable." Lincoln glared at his brother. "This is why I think you're not ready. You can't talk to people like that."

"It worked, didn't it?" Collin scowled, then headed out through the door of the lodge.

Cora avoided Lincoln as she casually walked in the direction of the kitchen. There was no doubt in her mind that Collin and Lincoln had some serious issues to work out. But that wasn't her focus at the moment. She needed to find out what Max knew about Billy and Kent. She also wanted to know what he was so desperate to go out and do. It certainly appeared as if he was lying about picking up more groceries.

"Excuse me, Max?" Cora ducked into the kitchen, just before the door could swing shut.

"Yes?" Max looked over at her, then frowned. "I'm a little busy."

"I know you are, and I don't mean to interrupt you." Cora watched as he picked up a knife and began to slice some celery. "Oh no, honey, doing it like that will take you forever." She walked over to the sink and washed her hands. "Here, I'll show you how to do it." She took the knife from him. "See, if you keep it going like this, you'll be done in no time." She sliced the knife through the celery stalks without ever fully lifting it off the cutting board.

"Wow." Max smiled as he looked up at her. "You're almost as fast as Billy."

"He's a great chef, isn't he?" Cora grabbed a few

more celery stalks. "It's a shame what they're doing to him. Acting as if he's some kind of criminal."

"It is." Max grabbed some potatoes and another knife. "He didn't like Kent much, but he sure didn't kill him."

"How come they didn't get along?" Cora nodded with approval as he began to swiftly slice through the potatoes.

"Before Kent came along, Billy was in charge of the kitchen. The last manager didn't say a word about what happened in the kitchen, because he trusted Billy to take care of it. But Kent, was different. I think he felt like he had something to prove, so he wanted to be in charge of everything. He said that Billy had to cooperate with him to keep everything running smoothly." Max shook his head. "But Billy wasn't interested in any of that."

"I can see how that would cause some serious friction." Cora switched over to peppers. "I heard they really had it out, not long before Kent was killed."

"They did, but actually, Kent apologized to him later." Max slid the potatoes into a container, then grabbed a few carrots. "I was surprised when he did. Billy and I were having a drink in the lobby bar, after it was closed to guests. Kent came in and paid for our drinks. He apologized to Billy for being so harsh with him. He said that Billy had been right about Collin getting the manager's job. He said he'd been on edge ever since Collin came back, because he was waiting to get replaced. But Billy tried to tell him that he was just upset because Kent told him what to do, he didn't mean what he said. He said that Lincoln was never going to go through with giving Collin, Kent's job. Lincoln didn't think that Collin had it in him. He partied all through hospitality school and barely graduated." He shrugged. "As far as I know, though, Collin was just waiting for the chance. I'd heard him talking to Penny about firing Kent, but I didn't tell Kent that. I didn't want him to worry."

"That was kind of you. I guess Kent wasn't such a bad guy, if he went out of his way to apologize." Cora set down her knife. "Did he have a drink with you two?"

"No, he didn't have a drink. He ordered one, but then a woman walked into the bar. One of the guests. Billy told her the bar was closed, but Kent excused himself and went over to talk to her. They left together after that." Max tipped his head toward the pile of vegetables she had sliced. "Thanks so much. I have to run to the drugstore. I need to pick up some medication for my mother."

"Oh, go on." Cora smiled. "I'll put these away." As she swept the vegetables into containers, she glanced around the kitchen. Nothing seemed out of place. When she had finished putting everything away, she stepped out of the kitchen.

Samantha took a step back as Cora emerged into

the hallway. "I saw someone in a kitchen uniform come out, and I thought you might be in there."

"You were right." Cora grinned. "You'd make a great detective."

"I don't know about that." Samantha sighed. "Things didn't go so well with Anne. But at least I found out she doesn't think Kent had anything to do with her accident. At least that's what she claims. They were good friends, and he asked her to come here for a reason, but he never had the chance to tell her what that reason was."

"I wonder if that's the truth." Cora leaned against the wall. "Because I have even more reason to believe now, that she's an absolute liar."

"Why do you say that?" Samantha perked up. "Did you find out something?"

"A few things, yes. Billy might not have had the motive that we first assumed, to kill Kent. It turns out that Kent actually went out of his way to apologize to Billy for the way he spoke to him. Max, who I just spoke to, was there with him when he did. But then Kent walked off with a woman, my guess is, it was Anne. But I didn't have the chance to find out for sure." Cora shook her head. "I don't know who else he would have walked off with."

"It could have been anyone here." Samantha frowned. "I don't think that we can assume that it was Anne."

"Max did say that it was a guest, and that she had

come into the bar after it was closed to guests for the night, specifically looking for Kent. I certainly don't think that we can rule out that it was Anne. Did you believe her when she said she didn't think Kent was involved?" Cora asked.

"I believed her. But as you said, she's lied to us already. Plus, she had her suitcases with her when I ran into her. She was returning to her room and claims that she was going to leave but decided to stay because she wants to find out what happened to Kent before she can move on. I don't know, something just doesn't add up to me." Samantha narrowed her eyes.

"Well, if she was the one who met with Kent, then she's lying about him not having the chance to talk to her. They obviously had time together." Cora nodded.

They turned to see Billy charging toward them.

"Billy, I thought the police had taken you away?" Cora called out. "I'm so glad you're free."

"They had to let me go because I didn't do anything wrong. They had nothing on me." Billy looked from her to Samantha, then walked past them toward the kitchen.

CHAPTER 19

"Let's go over what we know about the actual murder." Cora steered Samantha down the hallway. "That might give us a clue who the murderer is."

"Kent was struck with a heavy object, then pushed. Which means whoever killed him, likely went there with the intention to commit the act. There didn't seem to be much of a struggle. Either the killer took him by surprise, or maybe, and I think this is more likely, Kent knew his killer, and didn't feel threatened by the person that walked up to him. The fact that he was comfortable in the murderer's presence, made him an easy target." Samantha walked beside her. "Which brings us right back to Anne."

"It does. I'd like to see if Lincoln or Penny have heard anything more from the police about the investigation." Cora looked at Samantha. "What do you think?"

"Good idea," Samantha agreed. "I also still want to find out about Kent's running partner, Nate. We haven't been able to track him down."

"You think he ran with his murderer?" Cora asked.

"Maybe." Samantha nodded. "I think Penny's out walking the dogs, I saw her go out the door with them. We could try to meet up with her, then strike up a casual conversation?" She narrowed her eyes. "What do you think?"

"I think I'd better change my shoes." Cora looked down at her heels.

After Cora had put on her sneakers, Samantha led the way out toward the lake, with Cora right behind her. Cora had her suspicions, and she had her own. But when it came down to it, they'd worked well together, and she was glad that she wasn't alone in her search to find Kent's murderer. She only hoped that they would be able to figure it out.

"There they are." Samantha pointed to Penny and the two dogs far ahead of them, near the lake. "But if we're going to catch up with them, we're going to have to run."

"Let's go!" Cora broke into a run without the slightest hesitation.

Samantha held back a groan as she ran after her. She definitely hadn't been focused on fitness over the past few years, and her body made that clear the moment she started to run. Despite Cora being far older than her, the woman managed to catch up with Penny very quickly. Samantha met up with the two of them a minute or so later. She rested her hands on her thighs and leaned forward as she tried to catch her breath.

"Samantha, are you okay?" Penny looked over at her as Cora petted the Labradoodles.

"Yes, sorry." Samantha gulped down another breath. "It's not easy keeping up with this one."

"I do a boot camp for seniors class every week. I never miss it." Cora beamed as she looked up from the two dogs. "It's so important to stay active and fit, isn't it, Penny?"

"Yes, it is." Penny smiled as she held tightly to the dogs' leashes. "It's been so much easier since Collin got these two. I used to dread the thought of exercise. Getting sweaty, and the aches and pains that go with it. But when Collin brought them home, and they needed walks to keep them happy, I found a new love for walking and running with them."

"You usually take them out in the morning, too, right?" Samantha straightened up, finally able to breathe again, though her chest remained tight.

"Yes, usually, but we missed this morning." Penny glanced down at the dogs. "In the morning they get a swim in the lake as well. We try and make the most of it, before it gets too cold. Lincoln never takes them out. I've told him to, but he's never been into exercise."

Penny scratched behind Bruce's ear. "They look forward to it so much, and so do I."

"Speaking of running. I heard something about a friend of Kent's, a running partner. Nate. Do you know him?" Samantha looked into her eyes.

"Yes, Nate ran with him most mornings." Penny pursed her lips, then stepped closer to the two women. "Just between us, apparently Nate is the number one suspect, at the moment. He was on that run with Kent this morning, and no one has seen him since. The police haven't been able to reach him to even discuss what happened. My guess is, they fought over something, and Nate killed him." She sighed. "I don't even like to think about it. But it's the only thing that makes sense. Why else wouldn't he come forward?"

"That's a very good question." Cora nodded. "And you have no idea where he is?"

"I know where he works. He was meant to work today, but he hasn't been there all day, so that's not very helpful." Penny shrugged. "I'm sure the police will catch up to him soon enough. He can't run forever. I better get going." She turned and walked off down the trail.

"Interesting." Samantha settled on a large rock beside the lake. "So, he's still missing."

"Yes. But does that make him the killer?" Cora looked out over the water. "Penny had a good point, though. Why else would he be on the run?"

"I think we should find out." Samantha ran her

fingers over her pants. "The two were friends. Why would he suddenly attack Kent? I would think Kent would notice if his friend brought something heavy, like a baseball bat, along for the run. Wouldn't you?"

"Yes. But it's possible something like a tree branch was used." Cora shrugged. "So, he had the opportunity, but no motive that we know of, but that still doesn't explain why he took off."

"Did he?" Samantha peered up at her. "The only thing we know for sure is that he's missing."

"True. What if the killer did something to him, too?" Cora's eyes widened.

"We'd better start digging and find out what we can." Samantha stood up and brushed some mud off the back of her pants. As her palms grazed through the gritty substance, she recalled the sensation of brushing mud from her shirt after Boomer jumped up against her. "Mud." She stared at her palm as some mud glistened in the sunlight. "Penny is a liar, too."

"What?" Cora looked over at her with wide eyes.

"Penny said that no one in her family had been out this morning, but when one of the dogs jumped up on me this morning, he had muddy paws. And he was wet as if he had been swimming." Samantha nodded.

"Which means that the dog must have been in the lake this morning!" Cora gasped.

"And if the dogs were in the lake, then someone had to be out there with them. When we found Kent's body, Lincoln and Penny didn't have the dogs with them. If Penny is the one that walks the dogs, it must have been her." Samantha's heart raced as she looked back toward the lodge. "She had to have lied about one of them being at the lodge, there's only one reason she would lie about that."

"Maybe not just one." Cora tilted her head from side to side. "We'll have to look into it more. Maybe there is more than one explanation. Maybe she actually didn't know Collin or Lincoln had left the lodge with the dogs. Maybe they took the dogs out and lied to her to cover their tracks."

"Maybe." Samantha clenched her jaw as she started back toward the lodge. "But apparently Lincoln doesn't walk them. Maybe she's the murderer, and she's just trying to cover her tracks."

"She doesn't strike me as a killer." Cora followed after her. "But I know, that doesn't mean much of anything. I'll see what more I can find out about her, and this morning. You dig more into Nate. The sooner we can find him, the sooner we'll figure this out."

CHAPTER 20

Cora knew the easiest way to find out the truth about a boss was to talk to their employees. She'd heard many stories over the years. She knew how owners covered up things and how employees loved to share rumors. As she headed for the employees-only section of the lodge, she recalled seeing a small lounge just beyond the sign. She guessed it was used as a break room for the resort's employees. As she neared it, she noticed a few people inside. Two young women, and an older man, all three in uniforms that bore the name of the resort. She tapped her knuckles lightly against the open door and smiled as the three looked up at her.

"I'm so sorry to interrupt you, when you're having a break." Cora stepped inside before they could stop her. "I just wanted to speak to you. I won't take long."

"Whatever you need." The older man stood up and

straightened his shirt. "All you have to do is ask."

"Oh, that is so very sweet of you." Cora batted her eyes at him as his lips spread into a warm smile. "Actually, that's why I wanted to see you all. I know this has been a difficult time with what happened to Kent, and I just wanted to thank you all for the wonderful job you're doing. I'm sorry I interrupted you, but I didn't know how else to get the message to you."

"Thank you." One of the young women smiled. "It's nice to be appreciated. We better get back to it." She gestured to the other woman, who followed after her. "We'll catch up with you later, Pat." She waved over her shoulder at the man.

"I told Kent we should have a report feedback questionnaire for the guests, so the staff can see what they are doing right as well as wrong." Pat nodded to Cora. "We used to have one at the inn, but Kent said that Lincoln and Penny didn't like the idea. I think they just never want to hear any negativity."

"The inn?" Cora asked.

"There was an inn at the bottom of the mountain that burned down a few years ago, shortly after this resort was built." Pat winced. "No one was hurt, but the place was destroyed, and the owners decided it wasn't worth it to rebuild. Luckily this resort offered all of us jobs."

"That's terrible." Cora frowned. "Did they find out how it started?"

"It was investigated, and although it was suspicious, nothing could be proven." Pat shook his head. "Rumor was that the owners torched the place to get the insurance, but I never believed that. The couple that owned the place, Stan and Jill, were lovely. They would never do anything like that. They loved running the inn. It was very successful. They paid very well and never charged very much for the rooms. They were devastated when the place burned down."

"Oh, that's terrible." Cora gasped. "I want to find out what really happened to Kent. Don't you?" She looked into his eyes.

"Of course I do. We all do. Don't think that any of us haven't considered that we might be next. If someone was after Kent, then maybe they only wanted to kill him specifically. But what if it was random?" Pat shook his head and rubbed the back of his neck.

Cora had never really considered that the killer might have had no connection or motive at all to kill Kent. She still thought it was more likely he was targeted. She wanted to try to get more information from Pat.

"I heard that there was some tension between Collin and Kent?"

"Yes, there was." Pat nodded. "Collin wanted Kent's job, but Lincoln and Penny wouldn't give it to him. Ever since their parents died, Lincoln and Penny have been close, but there is tension with Collin." He lowered his voice as he stepped closer to her. "You didn't hear this from me, but they have their reasons for not making Collin the manager here. It's not because they don't love him. It's because they want what's best for him."

"How could giving away his job be what's best for him?" Cora narrowed her eyes. "It seems like he really wants that job."

"Well, Collin had a drinking problem. He took a break from hospitality school and went to rehab. He's had a drinking problem for a few years now and even totaled his car a while back. Luckily, he didn't hurt anyone or himself. But Penny put her foot down and sent him to rehab. I guess she's scared that making him manager would put too much pressure on him. He might not be able to handle it, and then he could end up back in rehab, or worse." Pat sighed as he folded his hands in front of him. "Trying to care for someone, being their guardian, isn't easy."

"That's very true." Cora's mind spun as she considered the possibility that Collin might have been involved in Anne's accident. It was a stretch, but if he had a history of alcoholism, and driving under the influence, then it was possible he was somehow connected. Was that why Kent had come to work at the resort? Did he suspect that Collin had a connection to Anne and their hometown tragedy? If so, and Collin found out, that would be even more motive to kill Kent before the truth could get out.

CHAPTER 21

Samantha looked at Nate's social media pages again and still found no posts from today. She sifted through the information and couldn't find a single hint as to where he might have gone, or why.

"This is getting me nowhere." She frowned as she closed her computer.

She decided the best way to find out more about Nate was to go to the hotel where he worked and see if any of his coworkers had an idea of where he might be. It felt a bit redundant as she was sure that the police had thoroughly questioned all of them, but she also knew that people often held back when it came to the authorities. His coworkers might be more forthcoming if she spoke to them.

Samantha hopped in her rental car and followed the directions to the hotel. She parked in the parking lot and looked through the windshield at the hotel. It looked quite expensive. As she stepped out of her car, her cell phone rang. At the sight of the name on the caller ID, she answered it.

"Mrs. Bing?"

"I went by your room, and when you weren't there, I decided to give you a call."

"I'm just at the hotel where Nate works. I'm about to go in and talk to some of his coworkers. Did you find out anything?" Samantha walked through the entrance of the hotel.

"I spoke to Pat who has worked at the resort one of the longest. He came from the inn that burned down." Cora told her what she had found out about the inn. "Pat told me that the reason Lincoln and Penny don't trust Collin to take over as manager is because he's had a drinking problem in the past. He did a stint in rehab. They're both concerned that the job would put too much pressure on him and cause him to backslide."

"Interesting." Samantha paused just inside the lobby of the hotel. "It makes sense that Collin might have still resented Kent. Which would still give him plenty of motive to go after someone he saw as a rival."

"He may have even more motive than that. Apparently, before he was sent to rehab, he was in an accident and totaled his car. I know it's just a hunch, but what if he's somehow connected to Anne's accident?" Cora's voice grew tight.

"Mrs. Bing!" Samantha gasped as she locked eyes with the man across from her. "It's him. He's here!"

"Nate?" Cora's voice snapped with surprise. "Are you sure?"

"Yes, I've been looking through his pictures. I know it's him." Samantha glanced away but kept him in her line of vision. Had he noticed her looking at him? "I'm going to see if I can talk to him."

"Samantha, don't you think we should call the police instead? They've been searching for him!"

"They won't be able to find him, if I let him disappear first! I'm going to follow him!" Samantha started down the hallway after him.

"Don't you dare hang up on me! I want to know what is going on! Samantha, you might be dealing with a killer!" Cora's voice raised.

"Shh! He'll hear you." Samantha kept the line connected but slipped her phone into her pocket as he turned a corner.

In a rush, as she didn't want to lose him, she turned the corner, and came face-to-face with him. His eyes locked on to hers and he scowled.

"Why are you following me?"

"Nate, I just want to talk." Samantha's heart pounded as she realized that Cora might have been right about her warning.

"Who are you?" Nate glared at her.

"I'm just trying to find out what happened to Kent." Samantha tried to sound casual in spite of her racing heart. "Where have you been? Why did you disappear?"

"I panicked." Nate balled his hands into fists. "I didn't know what to do. Kent and I were out on our usual run, we always started out together. But because of the injury to his leg, he had to go slower. So, I would run ahead and double back and meet him near the end of the trail, so we could finish together. When he didn't show up, I went back to find him, but I didn't go back that far. I thought maybe his leg was sore, and he didn't finish the run. He'd done that before. Then when I heard what happened to him, I knew if anyone found out that we had been on a run together, they would blame me, so I ran. I panicked." He shook his head. "I know it was stupid. I didn't know what else to do. I'm out of money, and I'm here to pick up the tips I left in my locker."

"Why would you run in the first place?" Samantha studied him. "Just because you were with Kent, that doesn't make you a suspect. You might have seen or heard something that could explain who killed him."

"Trust me, I will be a suspect." Nate met her eyes. "There are things in my past, things that will make it seem like I'm a terrible person. But I'm not. Kent knew that." He took a slow breath. "He was a good friend."

"I'm sorry that you've lost him." Samantha took a slight step back as she observed the genuine grief in his expression. No matter what was in his past, it still seemed strange to her that he would go into hiding after his friend's death, if he wasn't the murderer. "It's the right thing to do, to turn yourself in to the police."

"I sure hope so. It's not like I have a choice. Word will get to them soon enough, once people see me here. I knew coming out to get the money would be risky, but I couldn't survive without it. Now, there's no point in running anymore." Nate crossed his arms as he stared at her. "I'm sure that you won't hesitate to call the police."

The door to the lobby swung open, and Detective Greg stepped inside, with a group of police officers behind him.

"I didn't call them." Samantha took another step back as she saw rage flash through Nate's eyes.

Nate lifted his hands into the air as Detective Greg approached him with his gun drawn.

Only then did Samantha remember that Cora was still on the line. She pulled her phone out of her pocket and put it to her ear. "Mrs. Bing, are you still there?"

CHAPTER 22

"I'm here." Cora tried to catch her breath as relief flooded her. Even though she'd been able to hear the entire conversation, she couldn't see whether Samantha was safe.

"Did you call the police?" Samantha's voice tightened.

"I did. What else was I supposed to do? He could have hurt you, Samantha!" Cora raised her voice. "Come back to the resort. It's pretty clear that the police have caught their killer."

"I'm not so sure about that." Samantha cleared her throat. "I'll be there soon. I'm sure I'll have to talk to the detective first. I'm in the middle of his investigation, yet again."

"I'll be here when you get here." Cora ended the call. As she stowed her phone in her purse, she noticed that her hands still trembled.

Fear had run through her when she heard Nate confront Samantha. "What I need is some candy and a cup of coffee," Cora mumbled as she glanced at the coffee maker in the room. She decided that she didn't want to fiddle with it. She wished she was in Blue River and she could just pop into Charlotte's Chocolate Heaven.

She stepped out of her room and headed to the lobby. She hoped that her instincts were right, that the killer had been caught. It made sense that Nate would be the one to have killed Kent, since he was the last one with him, and he ran rather than face the police. What could be so terrible in his past that he wanted to avoid the authorities? She was almost to the kitchen, when she noticed a familiar face heading for the front door. Anne, carrying two suitcases.

"Anne." Cora's heart skipped a beat. Even though she believed that Nate might be the killer, she didn't want Anne to vanish before they had the chance to confirm it.

Anne ignored her as she continued toward the door.

"Anne, wait." Cora hurried over to her. "I have good news. I think the police have taken Kent's killer into custody."

"What?" Anne blinked, then took a sharp breath. "Seriously?"

"His friend, Nate, has been arrested, the one who he was supposed to be running with. I'd say there is a good chance that he's the killer." Cora searched her eyes. "Aren't you relieved?"

"Relieved? No." Anne narrowed her eyes. "There were so many times after my accident that we thought we had found the right person, but it always turned out not to be true. I'll be relieved when he's actually convicted and behind bars."

"But you won't be here to see that?" Cora gestured toward the suitcases.

"It's time for me to go. There's nothing here for me anymore. Kent's not here." Anne started toward the door again.

"I think we need to get a few things straight, first, Anne." Cora blocked the younger woman's way as she attempted to walk past her. It seemed strange to her that Anne would be in such a hurry to leave. Now that an arrest has been made, wouldn't she still want to stick around to see how it played out?

"I don't have to tell you anything." Anne narrowed her eyes as she stepped back away from Cora.

"You're right, you don't have to. But I'm not going to stop asking. So, wouldn't it be easier just to tell me the truth right now, so that we don't have to waste time on going back and forth?" Cora looked straight into her eyes. "Don't we want the same thing, to find out who killed Kent? And maybe somehow find out who caused your accident?"

"Yes, of course." Anne nodded.

"I know that you and Kent talked, even though

you said you never got the chance to. I know that you didn't stay here after Kent's death, just to find out what happened to him. There's more, isn't there?" Cora continued to hold the other woman's gaze. "Anne, just tell me the truth. If I can help you, I will."

"Help me?" Anne gave a short laugh as she looked up at the ceiling. "Oh, you think you can help me?" She looked back at Cora. "Can you make me play the piano again, like I used to? Can you bring Kent back? No, you can't, can you? So, no, you can't help me."

"Maybe not, but I can help you figure all of this out. You don't have to be alone in all of this." Cora's voice softened some as she leaned closer to Anne. "Listen, if Kent is the one who hit you, and you killed him, a judge and jury would understand what happened. It's better to tell the truth now, than to try to run or hide from it."

"Do I look like I'm running or hiding? I'm leaving! I'm leaving before all of this gets any worse!" Anne's eyes narrowed and her voice hardened. "I had nothing to do with Kent's death." Her voice faltered some.

"You don't really believe that, do you?" Cora took a sharp breath. "You do feel responsible, don't you? I can hear it in your voice."

"You're wrong." Anne shook her head.

"I only want one thing, Anne. I want to know what happened to Kent. We both do. I can see that now. I'm just trying to piece all of this together, with so little information. Can't you tell me anything about what you and Kent talked about?" Cora could feel she was getting through to the woman.

"There's nothing to tell." Anne sighed. "At least, not enough. He told me last night that he knew who had hit me, and that was why he brought me here."

"He did?" Cora's eyes widened.

"Yes. As soon as he told me that, I got upset. I wanted to know who it was. I demanded that he tell me. He got nervous, said he didn't want me to do anything stupid, and that he'd tell me when I'd had some time to calm down. He said he was close to getting the person to confess, he just needed a little more time." Anne gulped down a breath.

"It's okay. It's understandable that you're upset." Cora nodded.

"If only I had been calm. If only I had listened to him, maybe he would have told me the person's name, maybe he would still be alive! So, yes, I do feel responsible for his death." Anne held her breath. "Because I'm pretty sure that whoever hit me, murdered him, and he was murdered because of what he knew, because he was trying to find out the truth for me."

"You shouldn't blame yourself. None of this is your fault." Cora met her eyes as she processed Anne's words. Should she believe her? "Don't you want to stay? You might be able to help the police with their investigation."

"I just want to get out of here. I've just told the

police here about my accident and my suspicions, so they know to look into a connection and where to reach me. I have to go." As Anne pulled the door open, Samantha stepped inside.

"Anne," Samantha called out as Anne walked straight past her.

CHAPTER 23

"She was in a hurry." Samantha looked over at Cora.

"She was." Cora quickly relayed their conversation. "Maybe we should try to stop her."

"No, let her go. She might be the murderer, but I doubt keeping her here will make a difference." Samantha cleared her throat as she caught sight of a man headed in their direction. "And I think we still have some stones that we haven't turned over. Nate is with the police right now, and if he did this, I'm sure they will get him to confess. But in case he didn't do this, we do know of someone else who had plenty of motive."

"Collin." Cora watched as he walked over to the front desk and spoke with a woman who stood behind it. "Yes, from what we know, he still had the most to lose, if Kent was still alive. I think it's time we confronted him about it once and for all. Maybe his reaction will tell us something."

"He's never going to open up, if we both gang up on him, though." Samantha watched as he glanced over at them. "You talk with him, I'll watch from afar. I might be able to notice something that you don't."

"All right, let's see what we can find out." Cora walked toward him.

Samantha hung back as she watched the pair greet each other. She already detected a level of tension in the way that Collin stood, his shoulders tight and his back rigid. After a brief exchange of small talk, Cora looked straight into his eyes.

"Did you see anything out of the ordinary this morning?" Cora asked.

"No, I wasn't even at the resort until later this morning." Collin crossed his arms. "I was with my girlfriend this morning, and the police have verified it."

"Girlfriend?" Cora stepped closer to him. "If you were with your girlfriend, why did Penny say you were at the lodge?"

"I don't know! I can never figure out what she's up to. She's always got an angle. She does everything for the business, really, pretending to care about her family. This resort is everything to her. Like when she promised me Kent's job, but then gave it away to supposedly teach me a lesson. I had counted on that job, it was the reason I went to hospitality school."

Collin balled his hands into fists. "Then she just ripped it away from me, like it was a favor she was doing for me. Why wouldn't that make me angry?"

"Angry at Kent?" Cora met his eyes. "Or angry at Penny?"

"What does it matter?" Collin shrugged. "All that matters is that I wasn't here. I've told the police that, too. Why do you think they haven't been hounding me? I have an alibi."

"Girlfriends lie, Collin."

"Look, I have to go." Collin held up his hands and took a step back. "I had nothing to do with what happened to Kent."

As Cora walked over to join her, Samantha watched Collin walk away. His stance had become more relaxed, if anything.

"Well, we know one person who is certainly lying. If Collin really wasn't at the lodge this morning, then Penny not only lied about him being here, but it also narrows down the possibilities of who could have taken the dogs for a walk. It must have been Penny, if Lincoln really doesn't walk them. Maybe she encountered Kent when she was walking the dogs." She pointed in the direction of a hallway. "There she goes, now. Let's take a shot at her."

"Good plan." Samantha nodded and followed after her.

They followed Penny to the end of the hallway,

where she turned, and stepped through a door onto a balcony.

"If it's okay with you, I'll take the lead on this one." Samantha looked over at Cora. "I think if I speak to her alone, she'll be more relaxed and tell me more."

"Sure." Cora stayed in the hallway. "I'll be here for backup."

"Thanks." Samantha stepped out onto the balcony that overlooked the lake as Penny surveyed an assortment of plants.

"Oh!" Penny glanced over her shoulder at Samantha. "You startled me." She gripped the spray bottle in her hand so tight that her knuckles turned white.

"I'm sorry." Samantha walked to the railing of the balcony and looked out over it. "What a beautiful view."

"Yes, it's quite beautiful." Penny plucked a few leaves from one of the plants. "I spend quite a bit of time out here, actually." She took a deep breath of the fresh air. "It's calming."

"The plants are also beautiful." Samantha turned her attention to the plants.

"It's one of my favorite areas." Penny laughed. "I love to grow things, to nurture them."

"Is that why you lied to the police about Collin?" Samantha peered at her. "Was it your way of nurturing him?"

"I don't know what you're talking about." Penny

rolled her eyes. "Obviously, you seem to think you know something."

"I do. I know that Collin wasn't at the lodge this morning when Kent died, even though you claimed he was." Samantha crossed her arms. "So, you lied."

"Okay, yes." Penny spritzed some water onto the plant. "I wasn't sure where Collin was, but I knew, of course, that he couldn't be involved in something like this. So, I told the police that he'd been home all morning. Is that so wrong?" She looked over at her. "I know, it's easy to judge me. But it's not like it changes anything. He had nothing to do with Kent's murder." She set the bottle down as she stared at Samantha. "It was a huge responsibility when our parents died to take care of Collin, but it has been our responsibility. I will do anything to protect him. He just sees it as overbearing, but I have to do what I have to do to protect him. If that means pretending he was at the lodge when he wasn't, so be it."

"Is that why you gave away his job as manager, to protect him?" Samantha narrowed her eyes. "It seems to have upset him quite a bit."

"Being in the position I've been in, having to take care of him since our parents passed is a thankless job. Completely thankless. He put our business in jeopardy when he got into that accident. We could have lost everything. It cost us an arm and a leg to get lawyers for him and to get him into that rehab. Then he thinks we're just going to hand over the most important position here?" Penny gave a short laugh. "Sure, I wanted to protect him, but I also wanted to protect our business."

"You would do whatever it takes to protect your business, wouldn't you, Penny?" Samantha took a step toward her.

"It's all we have left." Penny shrugged. "We put every penny into this place. It can't fail. It was all the money my parents left us. I can't let everything we worked for be taken away." She stopped as her phone rang in her pocket. "I have to take this." She pulled her phone out of her pocket and stepped into the building.

Samantha followed her through the door. As she stepped through the doorway, Lincoln stepped in front of her path.

"Sorry." Samantha took a step back, startled by his sudden presence.

"Oh, Samantha, I wanted to show you something. A memorial I've created for Kent. I'd love to have your opinion on it, as a representative of the media. Would you mind?" Lincoln gestured toward some stairs.

"Sure, I'd love to take a look." Samantha smiled as she followed after him. She saw Penny continue down the hall as Cora walked over to Samantha. "Oh, Mrs. Bing should come, too. She's an expert on these types of things."

Cora's eyes widened. She had no idea what

Samantha was referring to, but she followed the two to the wooden stairs.

"It's just here." Lincoln started down the stairs. "Not even Penny knows about it, yet. I wanted to make sure that I had it just right." He turned toward them as they reached the bottom and stepped into the backyard. "I'm sure you will both appreciate it."

Samantha couldn't see any memorial. There were no flowers or anything, just lawn with an area in the corner that was surrounded by a tall chain-link fence. It looked like it was used to store gardening equipment.

"It's just over here." Lincoln led them to the fenced-in area of the yard. "We keep the gardening tools in here, so the dogs can't get to them. Excuse the mess."

"I don't see any mess." Cora peered through the gate at the assortment of equipment. She suddenly felt a hard shove from behind her. She heard Samantha gasp at the same moment and saw her stumble forward ahead of her.

"I do." Lincoln's voice hardened. "I see a very big mess. Luckily, I'm going to clean it right up."

Lincoln swung the gate shut and fastened the padlock, before Cora or Samantha could say another word.

CHAPTER 24

"Lincoln?" Cora stumbled forward another step and bumped into Samantha.

Samantha curved her hand around the other woman's elbow to steady her.

"What are you doing?" Samantha slammed her hand against the gate. "Let us out of here!"

"Sorry, I can't do that." Lincoln folded his arms as he peered at the two. "With all of your snooping, all of your questions, I guess that you figured a few things out."

Samantha's heart pounded as she realized that Lincoln had to be the killer. Although she had suspected that Penny might be involved, she hadn't really considered Lincoln.

"No, we haven't," Samantha whispered. "Is this because you're trying to protect Collin because he killed Kent? Because you gave him his job?"

"Wow, you two really didn't have it figured out, did you?" Lincoln scowled.

"Just let us go." Cora walked up to the gate as well. "We can let all of this be a memory. No one has to get hurt or arrested. We can just go back home."

"Sure you can." Lincoln sighed. "Wow, I guess I gave you two too much credit. Here I thought you were sniffing around Penny because you'd found some evidence against me and wanted her to confirm it. But no. Wait, tell me the truth, did you think it was Nate? Because I really worked hard to pin this on him. He deserved it, anyway."

Samantha swallowed hard. "Why do you say that?"

"Haven't you figured that out, either?" Lincoln laughed, then shook his head. "Kent fancied himself a detective, too. He'd followed a suspicion here, that's why he took the job with us. He confided to me one night that he was on a hunt for a hit-and-run driver that had hurt his friend, and that he believed he had found that person."

"He did?" Samantha's eyes widened.

"Yes." Lincoln nodded. "Nate."

"So, you framed Nate to take the fall? You killed Kent?" Samantha gasped. "But why?"

"You see Kent was very helpful, but very nosy." Lincoln clucked his tongue. "What I didn't know when I told him he could use one of the storage rooms and turn it into an office was that, when he was tidying it, he would find an old laptop. A laptop I had told Penny to get rid of. He decided to look through it and found searches about fire accelerant. About the owners and staff of the inn that burned down. The media reports about the inn burning down. Just a very nosy fellow, he was. He quickly put two and two together."

"He worked out you burned down the inn?" Samantha gasped.

"He did. You see, I had to get rid of the opposition, so this resort would be successful. I had no choice. Getting rid of the inn was the aim, getting the staff from the inn was a bonus." Lincoln glanced at the ground and shook his head. "Kent was going to go to the police. I wanted to try to pay him off to keep him quiet, but I just didn't have the money. We're practically broke. The resort costs a lot to maintain. And we had to pay all of Collin's fines and lawyers' fees, and the hefty cost of that fancy rehab we sent him to. But I knew I had to do something." He pulled his shoulders back. "I waited for Nate and him to go on their usual morning run and took my opportunity to frame Nate. You should have seen how surprised Kent was when I showed up with a baseball bat." He laughed, then shook his head. "People underestimate how far someone will go to protect their kingdom."

"You killed him in cold blood?" Cora asked in disbelief.

"Surprised?" Lincoln smiled as he stepped back

from the gate and smiled. "I don't blame you. I surprised myself. In fact, all of this time I've been trying to convince myself that it never happened. But it did." He looked straight into Cora's eyes. "What's done is done, and I did it. Once I realized that, I realized something else." He pulled a knife from the pocket of his vest and held it out in front of him. "I can do it again."

"Lincoln!" Samantha gasped. "You can't really believe that you'll get away with three murders. You can't possibly believe that! If you hurt us, then you're going to prison for sure!"

"Actually, the only way I'm going to prison for sure, is if I let the two of you live." Lincoln raised his eyebrows. "So, I'm left with no choice. You can scream and holler as much as you want, no one can hear you. Please don't think it's anything personal. I just can't let everything I've built be ruined. Otherwise I would never think of harming you."

"Please, Lincoln." Cora rattled the gate. "We won't tell anyone. We'll help frame Nate. He's the one that deserves to go to jail. He's the one that hurt an innocent girl and ran away. You did what you had to do. All you have to do is let us go, and we'll back up your story about him."

Samantha's chest tightened at the thought, but she knew that Cora was doing her best to save their lives.

"She's right. We'll make sure that he gets the blame for all of this. We can be your allies."

Samantha took a shaky breath as she tried to sound convincing.

"Lincoln?" Penny called out from the stairs. "Lincoln, are you down here?"

"Help!" Samantha shouted and slammed her hands against the gate. "Help us, please!" Her heart pounded against her chest. There was only one chance that they would be rescued. If Penny found them, she would surely let them go. She wouldn't want to be involved in a murder, or three. "Penny!" She banged the gate again as she saw Penny walk toward them.

"Over here!" Lincoln smiled.

CHAPTER 25

"What is going on here?" Penny walked toward the fence, her eyes wide and her voice raising with every word she spoke.

"These two bit off more than they could chew." Lincoln looked over at Penny. "So, now, we're going to have to get rid of them."

"Get rid of them?" Penny's voice trembled. "You must be joking."

"No, I'm not joking. They know everything." Lincoln looked into her eyes. "It's either them or us now."

"How could you do this?" Penny looked from Lincoln to Samantha and Cora. "Why would you trap them in there? How are we going to explain this?"

"We're not going to explain this." Lincoln pressed the knife into her hand. "You're going to kill them, we're going to dispose of their bodies in the lake. It's what needs to be done."

"Lincoln, no!" Penny gazed at him, horrified as the knife fell from her hand. "I won't do that. I can't do that."

"Why not?" Lincoln snatched the knife from the ground. "I had to kill Kent because of you, didn't I?"

"You never had to do that!" Penny raised her voice. "You never had to kill anyone!"

"You left me no choice." Lincoln cleared his throat. "Don't forget that you're the reason we're in any of this mess. You're the one that didn't get rid of that stupid laptop like I told you to. You're the one that does everything so sloppily that you let Kent find out what I had done. I did what I had to do to protect us, and now you're going to have to do the same thing. It's about time you took responsibility as our sister. It's about time you did something to protect our business." He pressed the knife into her hand again. "I know it isn't easy. It wasn't easy for me, either. But once you do it, you'll see, it's not so bad. All of our problems will go away." He shrugged. "You need to help me. I can't do it alone. Let's just get it done quickly, and we'll have all of this settled by dinner."

"Lincoln," Penny whispered his name as she stared at him. "We don't have to do this. We can just go. Right now. We can leave them here. We'll get a head start. We can leave the country, start over somewhere new." She managed a small smile. "A new start!"

"A new start?" Lincoln growled. "I have done everything to keep this resort, to make it a success. And you want me to leave it behind? We're practically broke, Penny! Thanks to you and Collin. We don't have any money to go to another country or start new lives. The only new place we'll be is behind prison bars."

"I have money!" Cora pushed against the gate. "I have money, and you can have all of it to make your getaway. Just let us go. Penny, you don't have to do this."

"Lincoln's right." Penny shook her head as tears streamed down her cheeks. "Lincoln's always been right. I never take care of things like I should, it's always Lincoln that has to do everything. But not this time. This time, I'm going to do things right. You can trust me, Lincoln." She looked over at her brother. "I will handle all of this."

"Good." Lincoln smiled. "I knew you had it in you, Penny."

Penny swallowed hard, then turned to face the gate. "I'm so sorry," she murmured as Lincoln released the padlock.

"Stay back!" Samantha stepped in front of Cora and pushed her to the side, so she was beside some of the gardening equipment. She hoped it would add more protection. "Don't even think of coming in here, Penny! I will make you regret it!"

As the gate swung open, Samantha felt a metal handle

being placed in her hand from behind. Before she knew what was happening, Cora ran past her and straight for Penny as she hoisted a shovel above her head. Before Penny could react, Cora swung the shovel down hard on top of Penny's hand that held the knife. The knife went flying straight toward the fence and out of her reach.

"Nice try," Lincoln growled as he charged toward Cora.

As he did, Samantha charged forward and slammed the shovel that Cora had placed in her hand, down on top of his head.

Lincoln crumpled to the ground with a groan as a loud voice called out, "Police! You're surrounded! Drop your weapons!"

It was only then that Samantha noticed a few police officers gathering at the bottom of the steps.

Samantha grabbed on to Cora's arm and pulled her close.

Cora held her breath as she watched the officers, led by Detective Greg, surge toward them.

Penny, who was sitting on the ground in a daze, held up her hands.

Lincoln lunged for the knife by the edge of the fence.

"You can't do anything right!" he huffed at his sister.

"Don't move!" Detective Greg shouted. "Lincoln, I will shoot, if you take another step closer to anybody.

You've done enough harm! It's time to surrender! Put your weapon down!"

"I'm so sorry. When Lincoln told me what he did, I had no choice. I had to try and protect him," Penny sobbed.

"You lied about your alibis to protect Lincoln?" Samantha asked.

"Yes, I soon realized that Lincoln must have been on the trail when I was walking the dogs. I tried to give us all alibis by saying we were at the lodge and no one took the dogs for a walk."

"Keep quiet, Penny! You'll ruin everything." Lincoln's voice trembled as he stared down the barrel of Detective Greg's gun. "It was Nate! He almost killed someone else and ran away before. Left her for dead. He's evil. It was Nate!"

"Nate told us all about that." Detective Greg took a step toward Lincoln. "Now, put down your weapon. This is your last warning."

Lincoln reluctantly released the knife, which fell to the ground.

Samantha breathed a sigh of relief.

Cora leaned into Samantha's side, breathless but grateful.

"Oh, thank you, Detective." Cora looked at him as officers handcuffed Lincoln and Penny.

"And I have Lincoln's confession on tape." Cora whipped out her phone with a wide grin on her face.

"You were amazing." Samantha looked at Cora. "Reckless, but amazing."

"Thank you." Cora smiled. "You weren't so bad yourself."

"How did you get the shovels?" Samantha asked.

"They were leaning against the lawn mower beside me." Cora looked down at the shovels, which had dropped on the ground. "He was so caught up with Penny, I managed to grab them. I knew I had to do something as soon as the gate swung open."

"Wow, you really do like getting into the middle of things." Detective Greg looked from Samantha to Cora.

"How did you know we were here? How did you know where to find us?" Samantha watched Penny and Lincoln being led away.

"Actually, you can thank Nate for that." Detective Greg looked them over. "Are you all right? Were you hurt in any way?"

"We're fine." Cora waved him away. "What were you saying about Nate?"

Samantha was in awe of Cora's strength, both physically and mentally.

"He confessed that he was involved in Anne's hit-and-run accident. He said he had been so drunk, he didn't even realize he'd hit someone, until he saw the news, and then the damage to his car. He panicked and ran." Detective Greg shook his head.

"But Kent knew?" Samantha asked.

"He suspected. Nate was staying in Bakersfield for a birthday party of a friend, and Kent was at the party as well. He had seen him drive off drunk. Kent recently confronted Nate about it. He admitted to Kent what he'd done. Kent convinced him that it was time to turn himself in." Detective Greg frowned. "Kent had called Anne here in the hopes of finding some closure for her by speaking to Nate."

"But he didn't turn himself in." Samantha raised her eyebrows.

"No, he didn't have a chance. When Kent's body was found, he was worried that everyone would believe he did it. He was the most obvious suspect, so he took off. He told us that Kent had confided in him about discovering information about Lincoln on an old laptop. Nate said when Kent turned up dead, he believed that Lincoln might have had something to do with it. We just found the laptop in Kent's car. We came to the resort looking for Lincoln, but he was nowhere to be found on the property."

"How did you find us?" Cora's eyes widened.

"Collin mentioned that he'd seen his brother, and the two of you, go down the stairs that led to the backyard. I had no idea that he had taken you both hostage, though." Detective Greg shook his head. "You both need to be a bit more careful in the future. You shouldn't get involved in things that don't concern you."

"Thanks for the advice, Detective." Samantha took

a deep breath. "But if we hadn't gotten involved, you might never have found out the truth about Kent's death, Lincoln's arson, or a young woman who was hit by a drunk driver."

"Yes, really you should be thanking us, since we did do your job for you." Cora walked beside him toward the stairs.

"Is that so?" The detective smiled.

"Not that we aren't grateful that you came to help us," Samantha added and shot a stern look in Cora's direction.

"We could have easily taken Lincoln and Penny down. We were just getting started." Cora smiled as she started up the stairs. "We make a great team. Don't we, Samantha?"

"That we do, Mrs. Bing." Samantha followed behind her. "That we certainly do."

With Kent's murder solved, Anne finally been given some closure for her accident, and the arson at the inn being solved as well, Samantha felt quite satisfied. It wasn't exactly the vacation that she had planned, but it had been quite productive.

"Does this mean we get some time in that indoor pool, now?" Cora glanced over at Samantha. "I'd love to get you out in the water to swim some laps."

"Lovely." Samantha winced. "That sounds just lovely."

"Don't worry." Cora patted her arm. "I won't let you drown, dear."

"Thanks." Samantha rolled her eyes.

"You should see Arnold, he can swim." Cora smiled. "You must come and meet him one day."

"Oh, I'd love to." Samantha nodded. "Maybe my friends from Sage Gardens will come with me, and we can get some of that delicious chocolate."

"Good plan." Cora reached into her purse and pulled out two milk chocolate caramels. She handed one to Samantha. "But there's no reason to wait, when we can have one now." She winked as she unwrapped the candy and popped it in her mouth.

The End

∼

Thank you for reading *Mayhem at the Mountain Resort*. I hope you enjoyed Mrs. Bing and Samantha's sleuthing adventure. If you want to read more cozy mysteries with them and their quirky friends, Mrs. Bing is from the Chocolate Centered Cozy Mystery Series and Samantha is from the Sage Gardens Cozy Mystery Series.

ABOUT THE AUTHOR

Cindy Bell is a USA Today and Wall Street Journal Bestselling Author. She is the author of over one hundred books in twelve series. Her cozies are set in small towns, with lovable animals, quirky characters, delicious food and a touch of romance. She loves writing twisty cozy mysteries that keep readers guessing until the end.

When she is not reading or writing, she loves baking (and eating) sweet treats or walking along the beach with Rufus, her energetic Cocker Spaniel, thinking of the next adventure her characters can embark on.

If you'd like to receive an email when she has a new release, please join her cozy mystery newsletter at https://www.cindybellbooks.com.

ALSO BY CINDY BELL

CHOCOLATE CENTERED COZY MYSTERIES

Chocolate Centered Cozy Mystery 10 Book Box Set (Books 1 - 10)

Chocolate Centered Cozy Mystery Series Box Set (Books 1 - 4)

Chocolate Centered Cozy Mystery Series Box Set (Books 5 - 8)

Chocolate Centered Cozy Mystery Series Box Set (Books 9 - 12)

Chocolate Centered Cozy Mystery Series Box Set (Books 13 - 16)

The Sweet Smell of Murder

A Deadly Delicious Delivery

A Bitter Sweet Murder

A Treacherous Tasty Trail

Pastry and Peril

Trouble and Treats

Fudge Films and Felonies

Custom-Made Murder

Skydiving, Soufflés and Sabotage

Christmas Chocolates and Crimes

Hot Chocolate and Homicide

Chocolate Caramels and Conmen

Picnics, Pies and Lies

Devils Food Cake and Drama

Cinnamon and a Corpse

Cherries, Berries and a Body

Christmas Cookies and Criminals

Grapes, Ganache & Guilt

Yule Logs & Murder

Mocha, Marriage and Murder

Holiday Fudge and Homicide

Chocolate Mousse and Murder

SAGE GARDENS COZY MYSTERIES

Sage Gardens Cozy Mystery 10 Book Box Set (Books 1 - 10)

Sage Gardens Cozy Mystery Series Box Set Volume 1 (Books 1 - 4)

Sage Gardens Cozy Mystery Series Box Set Volume 2 (Books 5 - 8)

Birthdays Can Be Deadly

Money Can Be Deadly

Trust Can Be Deadly

Ties Can Be Deadly

Rocks Can Be Deadly

Jewelry Can Be Deadly

Numbers Can Be Deadly

Memories Can Be Deadly

Paintings Can Be Deadly

Snow Can Be Deadly

Tea Can Be Deadly

Greed Can Be Deadly

Clutter Can Be Deadly

Cruises Can Be Deadly

Puzzles Can Be Deadly

Concerts Can Be Deadly

MADDIE MILLS COZY MYSTERIES

Maddie Mills Cozy Mysteries Books 1 - 3

Slain at the Sea

Homicide at the Harbor

Corpse at the Christmas Cookie Exchange

Lifeless at the Lighthouse

Halloween at the Haunted House

DUNE HOUSE COZY MYSTERIES

Dune House Cozy Mystery Series 10 Book Box Set (Books 1 - 10)

Dune House Cozy Mystery Series 10 Book Box Set 2 (Books 11 - 20)

Dune House Cozy Mystery Series Boxed Set 1 (Books 1 - 4)

Dune House Cozy Mystery Series Boxed Set 2 (Books 5 - 8)

Dune House Cozy Mystery Series Boxed Set 3 (Books 9 - 12)

Dune House Cozy Mystery Series Boxed Set 4 (Books 13 - 16)

Seaside Secrets

Boats and Bad Guys

Treasured History

Hidden Hideaways

Dodgy Dealings

Suspects and Surprises

Ruffled Feathers

A Fishy Discovery

Danger in the Depths

Celebrities and Chaos

Pups, Pilots and Peril

Tides, Trails and Trouble

Racing and Robberies

Athletes and Alibis

Manuscripts and Deadly Motives

Pelicans, Pier and Poison

Sand, Sea and a Skeleton

Pianos and Prison

Relaxation, Reunions and Revenge

A Tangled Murder

Fame, Food and Murder

Beaches and Betrayal

Fatal Festivities

Sunsets, Smoke and Suspicion

Hobbies and Homicide

Anchors and Abduction

Friends, Family and Fugitives

LITTLE LEAF CREEK COZY MYSTERIES

Little Leaf Creek Cozy Mystery Series 10 Book Box Set (Books 1-10)

Little Leaf Creek Cozy Mystery Series Box Set Vol 1 (Books 1-3)

Little Leaf Creek Cozy Mystery Series Box Set Vol 2 (Books 3-6)

Little Leaf Creek Cozy Mystery Series Box Set Vol 3 (Books 7-9)

Little Leaf Creek Cozy Mystery Series Box Set Vol 4 (Books 10-12)

Little Leaf Creek Cozy Mystery Series Box Set Vol 5 (Books 13-15)

Chaos in Little Leaf Creek

Peril in Little Leaf Creek

Conflict in Little Leaf Creek

Action in Little Leaf Creek

Vengeance in Little Leaf Creek

Greed in Little Leaf Creek

Surprises in Little Leaf Creek

Missing in Little Leaf Creek

Haunted in Little Leaf Creek

Trouble in Little Leaf Creek

Mayhem In Little Leaf Creek

Cracked in Little Leaf Creek

Stung in Little Leaf Creek

Scandal In Little Leaf Creek

Dead in Little Leaf Creek

Scared in Little Leaf Creek

Felled in Little Leaf Creek

Deceit in Little Leaf Creek

Secrets in Little Leaf Creek

Poisoned in Little Leaf Creek

Silenced in Little Leaf Creek

DONUT TRUCK COZY MYSTERIES

Deadly Deals and Donuts

Fatal Festive Donuts

Bunny Donuts and a Body

Strawberry Donuts and Scandal

Frosted Donuts and Fatal Falls

Donut Holes and Homicide

WAGGING TAIL COZY MYSTERIES

Wagging Tail Cozy Mystery Box Set Volume 1 (Books 1 - 3)

Murder at Pawprint Creek (prequel)

Murder at Pooch Park

Murder at the Pet Boutique

A Merry Murder at St. Bernard Cabins

Murder at the Dog Training Academy

Murder at Corgi Country Club

A Merry Murder on Ruff Road

Murder at Poodle Place

Murder at Hound Hill

Murder at Rover Meadows

Murder at the Pet Expo

Murder on Woof Way

Murder at Beagle Bay

NUTS ABOUT NUTS COZY MYSTERIES

A Tough Case to Crack

A Seed of Doubt

Roasted Peanuts and Peril

Chestnuts, Camping and Culprits

BEKKI THE BEAUTICIAN COZY MYSTERIES

Hairspray and Homicide

A Dyed Blonde and a Dead Body

Mascara and Murder

Pageant and Poison

Conditioner and a Corpse

Mistletoe, Makeup and Murder

Hairpin, Hair Dryer and Homicide

Blush, a Bride and a Body

Shampoo and a Stiff

Cosmetics, a Cruise and a Killer

Lipstick, a Long Iron and Lifeless

Camping, Concealer and Criminals

Treated and Dyed

A Wrinkle-Free Murder

A MACARON PATISSERIE COZY MYSTERY

Sifting for Suspects

Recipes and Revenge

Mansions, Macarons and Murder

HEAVENLY HIGHLAND INN COZY MYSTERIES

Murdering the Roses

Dead in the Daisies

Killing the Carnations

Drowning the Daffodils

Suffocating the Sunflowers

Books, Bullets and Blooms

A Deadly Serious Gardening Contest

A Bridal Bouquet and a Body

Digging for Dirt

WENDY THE WEDDING PLANNER COZY MYSTERIES

Matrimony, Money and Murder

Chefs, Ceremonies and Crimes

Knives and Nuptials

Mice, Marriage and Murder

Printed in Great Britain
by Amazon